About the Author

Born in North Yorkshire, I eventually qualified as an engineer and lecturer. I have worked for a number of colleges and engineering companies. My home is now in West Yorkshire, where I live with my wife Joan and our dog Rosie. We have three children and six grandchildren, who all live in the same area.

Brave and Industrious

B. E. Turner

Brave and Industrious

Vanguard Press

VANGUARD PAPERBACK

© Copyright 2024
B. E. Turner

A CIP catalogue record for this title is
available from the British Library.

ISBN 978 1 80016 866 4

*Vanguard Press is an imprint of
Pegasus Elliot Mackenzie Publishers Ltd.*
www.pegasuspublishers.com

First Published in 2024

**Vanguard Press
Sheraton House Castle Park
Cambridge England**

Printed & Bound in Great Britain

In memory of a brave and industrious people who helped to make Britain a world industrial leader.

Acknowledgements

My thanks to all at Pegasus Publishers for their help and assistance in producing this book. Thanks to my wife Joan and family for their encouragement.

Chapter 1
1815

Although the Industrial Revolution had started in Great Britain in the 1780s, it was not fully felt until the 1830s, when almost every aspect of daily life would be influenced in some way. Many of the technological inventions and innovations were of British origin, marking a turning point in history. The standard of living for the general population would increase consistently for the first time and give young people new opportunities.

At this time, most of the reasonably well-off families would expect their sons to have a career in politics, the church or the armed forces; their daughters would expect to be married to a suitably well-off gentleman. Things, however, would change, giving rise to new occupations in engineering and manufacturing.

The Battle of Waterloo was fought on Sunday 18th June 1815 near Waterloo in Belgium, and would see the final defeat of the French army under the command of Napoleon Bonaparte. Two armies of the British-led coalition, with the Duke of Wellington in command and the Prussian army under the command of Field Marshal von Blücher, would defeat Napoleon's army and mark the end of the Napoleonic Wars.

Many of the regiments who fought at Waterloo had been involved in fighting the French in the Peninsular War, which featured brutal guerrilla warfare and lasted six years.

The Battle of Leipzig in October 1813 had seen the defeat of Napoleon, forcing his abdication in April 1814. Napoleon was exiled on the island of Elba, which is between Corsica – where he was born – and Italy. However, he escaped from Elba in February 1815 and took control of France, which ultimately led to his final defeat at Waterloo. The British exiled him to the remote island of Saint Helena in the South Atlantic, where he died in 1821 at the age of fifty-one.

Six brave young men who fought in the Battle of Waterloo would later have sons who would become great friends, although they did not know this until later. They were not aware of each other; each was in a different cavalry regiment and came from different locations across the United Kingdom. They were all loyal to their country and king, George III (1760 to 1820), whom they served with distinction.

Fergus McDonald, a captain in the 2nd British Dragoons (Scots Greys) was sent in with his platoon to attack and delay the massed ranks of the French advance guard. The cavalry charge managed to force back the foot soldiers, savagely cutting them to pieces once they had fired their muskets. Many men died on both sides;

however, the Scots were at an advantage until the French lancers were sent in to the slaughter, outnumbering them. The recall was sounded for the Scots to get back to their own lines. Fergus held back part of his troop, allowing the rest to retreat. They fought bravely, but a lancer caught Fergus a glancing blow to his leg, which split open; however, he managed to turn and slash the man's arm with his sabre and shout, "Every man for himself! Get back to our lines!"

They rode back, pursued by the lancers, but some of his troop could not make it and were killed, while Fergus and the others made it to the British lines. The lancers had to retreat as the cannon and musket fire supporting the Scots Greys was cutting them down. The wound Fergus had received was nasty; it was cleaned and dressed and he was sent back behind the lines to eventually recover in Scotland.

On the second day of battle, Marshal Ney of France sent in his massed cavalry in an attempt to finish off the British infantry. Wellington formed his force into massed squares to be able to fire from four sides, bringing down men and horses. This was a mistake by the French, who lost many of their best cavalry units.

Henry Armstrong, an officer in the 1st Regiment of Life Guards, and Samuel Brown, an officer in the 1st Royal Dragoons, were being held in reserve by Wellington as the battle raged. At a vital point, to rout the French cavalry, the two regiments were sent in to attack from both sides in a pincer movement. Both Henry and

Sam were caught up in hand-to-hand fighting, which was brutal; however, to save some of their men, the French called a retreat, and the battle was over for the many dead and dying. Henry had a slight arm wound, while Sam was untouched, and both survived the battle and were ready for a rest.

The final day of the battle arrived bright and sunny after a tremendous downpour during the night. Although the field of battle was a muddy mess, Napoleon sent in his best infantry to attack the British middle ground prior to a cannon bombardment. This nearly succeeded, but for the British light cavalry attacking the left flank and the Prussians under Von Blücher arriving to attack the right flank.

Captain Edward Shawcroft was commanding the 16th (Queens) Light Dragoons and Lieutenant Robert Cromwell the 11th Light Dragoons as they charged into the French side. Many men died from musket shot before they reached Napoleon's Old Guard.

Robert Cromwell was hit in the chest, fighting on bravely and cutting down men as he advanced. Unfortunately, he fell from his horse and was bayoneted. His wounds, however, were not fatal, and after receiving emergency treatment in a field hospital, was sent home to recover. His military service was over.

Edward Shawcroft, attacking wildly with his troop, managed to slice many French down in a bloody mêlée. He was getting into difficulty as a French Lancer was about to unhorse him, after the Lancers had made a charge with depleted numbers. Jack Archer, who was Edward's Sergeant Major, saw the danger and managed to deflect the lance away and cut down the Lancer, at the same time being wounded by a French Guard. The action earned Jack a medal and the grateful thanks of his Captain whose life he had saved. Edward and Jack survived the battle and would become close friends for life.

The French were defeated at the Battle of Waterloo, which was Napoleon's last. Wellington was heard to say, "The battle was the nearest-run thing you ever saw in your life." He became a great British hero. This ended the First French Empire and began decades of relative peace, however at great human cost. It is estimated that the French had forty-one thousand casualties and the British twenty-four thousand casualties – this included those killed, wounded or missing. On both sides, a total of seven thousand horses were killed; a terrible loss, as horses were used for many purposes, including transport.

The Battle of Waterloo on land and the Battle of Trafalgar at sea (1805) were great British victories which ultimately defeated the French. This produced two leaders remembered now: The Duke of Wellington and Lord Nelson.

Chapter 2
1830

In 1830, King William IV came to the throne. However, he was an old man by then and would die in 1837. The new monarch was Queen Victoria, who would reign for nearly sixty-four years.

The six young Cavalry officers who had fought bravely at Waterloo would all have sons born in 1830. All the boys, as they grew up, would be taught by their fathers how to ride well and the art of sword fencing, self-defence and the use of firearms.

Fergus McDonald married Jean Stewart and lived in his family home, Ormiston Hall, south of Edinburgh. They had two daughters: in 1830, Ann was six years old and Ruth four years. On 20th April, a little boy was born who they named Angus.

Fergus had retired from the army and invested in two business ventures, the first in mining coal in the area and the other in textile manufacture. Both would become worthwhile to the future survival of the family. Angus grew up to be a strong boy and was eventually sent to school in Edinburgh.

On 3rd March, a son, George, was born to Henry and Mary Armstrong, who lived in Belsay Hall in Northumberland. Henry, who had left the army after his father's death, was now running the new engineering company his father had founded. They would go on to have two more children, a boy and a girl. George, the eldest, was a bright boy and as he grew became very interested in the new steam engines. He went to school in Newcastle.

Samuel Brown was now a senior staff officer with a wife, Claudia, and having seen her give birth to three girls, was overjoyed to see the birth of a son on 28th May. The new baby was called William, after the old king. They lived in Bridge Manor near Ironbridge, Wrekin; this is where the first iron bridge was built. Once grown into a sturdy little lad, he was often in the company of his grandfather John, who had set up one of the first iron foundries. When his father was at home, which was often now there was peace with the French, he would be taught by him. He was sent to Rugby School to finish his school years.

Edward and Melissa Shawcroft lived in Chard House near Chard in Somerset, which was a large family estate. The family wealth had come from their shipbuilding company founded by great grandfather Edward. A large estate needed many servants, the house had many horses and a separate large stable to accommodate the horses and many carriages. The present stable manager was ready to retire, so Edward had asked his army sergeant

Jack Archer to take on the position, an excellent choice for a retired cavalry dragoon. Both Edward and Jack had now left the Army, Edward to go into the family business and Jack who was happy to take on the job of Stable Manager. On 5th June, Melissa gave birth to their first child, Frederick. Not long after this, Jack, who had married his childhood girlfriend Molly, would see the birth of his son Peter on 8th June.

The two boys grew up together and, like their fathers, became close friends. Although both boys grew to be good sportsmen, Peter turned out to be much the cleverer of the two. Edward had arranged to have them both tutored together, and when they were old enough sent them both to school in Bath.

Robert Cromwell, who had been badly wounded at Waterloo, had to retire from the Army. He now ran his family estate, Longmeadows, near Midhurst in Sussex, which included the management of a number of farms. Just before Waterloo, he had married Alice Middleton, and when his son John was born on 2nd July, he already had a daughter June, who was now nearly two. John soon grew up to be a bright, active boy, who loved helping on the estate, often visiting the tenant farms. The outdoor life was far more interesting to him, although he managed to complete some tutoring and was then sent to school in London to finish his elementary education.

In the early years of the Industrial Revolution most poor children got no education, while those from the upper class were sent to fee-paying public schools. Only boys were sent away to school; girls from the upper class would often be taught at home.

Robert Raikes initiated the Sunday School movement in Gloucester in 1780. The teaching was mainly from the bible, and the children were taught to read and write. At this time, some children were fortunate in their education; many would never read and write. It was not until 1839 that the first schools termed Ragged Schools were established. Thomas Guthrie started the first school in Edinburgh. Anthony Ashley Cooper, 7th Earl of Shaftesbury, formed the Ragged School Union for poor children, which led eventually to the schools we have today. Girls would gradually be given an education, but it was not until 1879 that women could attend higher education.

Angus McDonald grew up with two big sisters, Ann and Ruth, who loved him and played with him as a toddler; he would call them Annie and Ruthie. From an early age they would learn to ride; when the girls were practising, Angus, a toddler, would shout, "I want to ride, too."

So Annie would say, "Come on then," and lift him up on her horse.

Soon, Angus would become an expert horseman; in fact, he was good at most things, although he would try to avoid his studies if he could.

Ormiston Hall lay south of the small village of Ormiston in East Lothian. It was the first planned village in Scotland, founded in 1735 by John Cockburn. Robert

Burns's nephew, William Begg, became the parish schoolmaster living in the schoolhouse with his family. He later moved to nearby Tranent in 1834, where he resigned his post and emigrated to America.

At the age of seven, Angus was sent to boarding school in Edinburgh. With some trepidation, he arrived by horse and carriage driven by his father Fergus, who said, "You are a very lucky boy to attend this new school. I expect you to do your best."

The school was Merchiston Castle School, founded by Charles Chalmers in 1833. It was the former home of John Napier, the inventor of logarithms. At first, Angus found the school rules rather hard and regimented, especially among a crowd of bigger boys, and he missed home. Soon, he settled down, making friends with boys in his year and his house and starting to enjoy the company of boys his own age. He would return home for holidays, when, during the summer break, he could ride his horse Chestnut, which his father had given him after a good school report.

One summer break, when Angus was sixteen years old, he decided to go riding in the Lammermuir Hills. On this occasion, he was startled when he saw a white mare who was stood neighing beside a path leading into a small wooded area. On reaching the horse, he could see a young girl about his own age lying on the ground in a state of shock, so he took a bottle of water from his saddlebag and gave her a drink. On recovering a little, she told him her name was Rose Laidlaw from Tranent House. Rose was a lovely girl, and Angus was immediately attracted to her. She told him how a deer had suddenly run out in front of them, causing her horse Snow to rear up, throwing her off. Now, she was nursing a bruised head but was otherwise all right. Angus helped her back on Snow. "I will see you safely back home," he said.

She replied, "That would be very good of you. I would welcome your help."

They chatted about almost everything, but in particular their love of horses, until they soon arrived back at Tranent House, where Rose said, "I feel fine now, but could you call again tomorrow and we can ride out together?"

"I would love to," said Angus.

So began a friendship which would lead to a close relationship, which blossomed every time Angus was at home, until they eventually fell in love.

On his eighteenth birthday, they were out riding and stopped to sit by the river, when Angus said to Rose, "I am afraid I will have to go away to University. My Father insists I go to one of the best, Cambridge."

Rose said, "I am happy for you; however, I do love you and wish I could go with you."

"I love you, too," said Angus. "I will come back home when I can. Will you wait for me so we can get married?"

"Do not talk of marriage yet," said Rose. "I am yours and I will wait for you, my love."

At this, they kissed, which led to an embrace and wild, eager lovemaking for the first time. Afterwards, Angus said, "I will ask your father if we could get engaged."

Rose was happy with that, and a week later Angus presented her with a lovely diamond engagement ring.

George Armstrong grew up in Belsay Hall with his little brother Graham and sister Jean. George was two years and three years older respectively. They were taught first by their Nanny Mrs Brown, who they loved. She had been their mother's Nanny and was part of the family since her husband, a butcher, had died. Later, they were taught by a Tutor, Mr Goodwin, who had studied at Cambridge. The boys were taught to ride, shoot and fence by their father when he was home from running his new engineering company in Newcastle. Henry would often stay in a house they had in Newcastle, which turned out to be useful when George was sent to the Royal Grammar School. He was able to go to the house each evening and ride home at the weekends. As time passed, George became very interested in his father's business and engineering production, so much so that his father recognised his ability and said to him, "Do well in Maths and Science and I will send you to one of the best Universities."

George said, "I will do my best; they are subjects I enjoy."

Although George was not that interested in girls at first, at the age of sixteen he did take a shine to one of his sister Jean's friends. Caroline was a very pretty girl who lived in the village; her father was the local doctor. As time passed, the children would all play and ride together, and George would enjoy returning home to see his family and in particular Caroline. He was not sure if Caroline felt as he did, so he said to Jean one day as they strolled in the grounds, "Do you think your friend Caroline likes me as I like her?"

"Of course she does, you silly, can't you tell?" replied Jean. "Ask her out, take her to the village inn."

George and Caroline met up at the inn and became close friends, often walking out or riding together in the Northumberland hills when George came home at the weekends. Soon, it was time for George to go to University. He had done well in his school work and had a good report which indicated his success as a sportsman and his scientific ability.

The three sisters of William Brown were April, May and June – their mother liked the idea of linking their names to the month they were born. William loved his sisters, although they tended to mother him, and as he grew, he would often escape with his grandfather to his foundry in Ironbridge Gorge. This is a deep gorge containing the River Severn in Shropshire formed by a glacial overflow at the end of the Ice Age. The deep exposure of the rocks cut through by the gorge exposed commercial deposits of coal, iron ore, limestone and fireclay, which enabled the economic development of the area during the early Industrial Revolution. It is often said to be the birthplace of Industry. William was very interested in the business and enjoyed working with his hands in the blacksmiths' shop. However, his father was keen he had a good education. His sisters taught him his basic subjects, after which he was sent off to Rugby School to, as his father said, "become a man".

At school, William, being a strong, robust boy, soon made his mark, and as time passed he became senior prefect. He would return home when he could, and although he had three sisters and met their friends, he never got romantically involved. April, his eldest sister, would introduce him to some young lady, then say, "Why don't you invite her out?"

His answer would be, "I am off to University soon, so I am not interested."

Frederick Shawcroft, usually shortened to Fred, was an only child and therefore was spoilt by his mother, who had a number of miscarriages and was advised to be careful in the future. Fred, however, was made to study and train with the son of his father's friend, Peter Archer; they both became very close and as they grew up were more like brothers. Peter had a little sister, Ellie, who also became part of the family, loved by them all. The boys had a great time growing up on a large estate, where they became good horsemen. After home tutoring, the time came for them to be sent away to school. Mrs Shawcroft was not happy with the situation; however, she was overruled by her husband, who said, "It is a family tradition that all the boys in the family be sent to school in Bath. A new school has opened in Bath, so I have arranged for their education there at the Prior Park Catholic College. They must do well and go to one of the best universities."

The two boys did do well at school; both were good at most subjects, Fred the better at most sports and Peter better academically. As time passed, they became good-looking young men, although Fred, with his blond hair and great physical attributes, was a born leader greatly admired by the girls. The boys would spend as much time as possible at home in Chard, where they would meet up with the girls from the village. Peter was keen on Jane Moore, who lived in the bakery. However, he was careful not to get too involved. Fred, on the other hand, got very involved with Melissa Osbourne, the vicar's daughter, a real beauty and very much taken with Fred. He unfortunately got her pregnant, which caused a problem which could not be tolerated due to the Shawcroft family being Catholics and a marriage being out of the question. Fred said to his mother, "I love her and I am willing to marry her."

But his mother said, "You must finish your education and then you may want to reconsider your situation."

Without telling her husband, arrangements were made with the vicar's wife to send Melissa away to get rid of the baby, and Fred had to say no more about it to anyone.

During this time, Fred spent some time at the family shipbuilding yard in Exmouth, where he became very interested in Naval Architecture. Chard claims to be the birthplace of powered flight, as it was here that the aeronautical pioneer John Stringfellow first demonstrated that engine-powered flight was possible through his work on the Aerial Steam Carriage. Peter got to know John and was often found helping him in his workshop, where he became fascinated with Aeronautics.

The boys' final reports from school were good: both did well in maths and science, which they needed to study one of the new science courses at University. Edward Shawcroft was delighted with them and took them to visit some of the local universities; a decision was then made after much discussion on their future education.

Midhurst is situated between the South Downs and the Low Weald in the county of Sussex, and in 1831 there were only forty-one eligible voters. It was near here that John Cromwell grew up on the family estate. He was descended from Oliver Cromwell, who was himself descended from Thomas Cromwell (a minister of Henry VIII).

Oliver Cromwell, who, in 1653, became Lord Protector of the Commonwealth of England, Scotland and Ireland, was known as the leader of the Roundheads. Roundheads were supporters of the Parliament of England during the English Civil War (1642-1651); they fought against King Charles 1st of England and his supporters, known as Cavaliers. Most Roundheads sought constitutional monarchy in place of absolute monarchy and the principle of the divine right of kings, and to this end to give Parliament supreme control over the executive administration of the country. At the end of the civil war in 1649, public antipathy towards the king was high, which led to his execution and allowed republican leaders to abolish the monarchy completely and establish the Commonwealth of England.

John spent his younger years being tutored with his sister June. However, as he got old enough to ride, he would be out at the many farms on the estate. He loved the countryside and was a little unhappy when he was sent off to school. Once he arrived at Charterhouse School in Smithfield, London, he soon settled in, showing talent both in the classroom and out in the playing fields. Charterhouse has a historic joint claim with Westminster School to having founded Association Football, which remains the main winter sport at the school. John found he was good at football and loved playing for the school. As time went by, he became head boy and was given good reports.

When he could get home, he would visit the farms, and he became very interested in the new agricultural machines and increasingly in a pretty farmer's daughter called Grace Croft. John would visit the Crofts' farm as soon as he could when he arrived home from school at the weekends. He would help Grace with the jobs around the farm, which led to them falling in love. The family were not too keen on the relationship; they hoped he would forget her when he went to university. John and Grace would often end up in the hayloft after mucking out the stables, but they had to be discreet to avoid being found out. It turned into a regular lovemaking session as they could not resist their passion for each other. John said to Grace, "I love you very much; will you marry me?"

Grace was overcome with emotion. "Yes, I adore you, but we had better wait for you to finish at the university before making any plans."

John became interested in the new farm machines being used, realising that they would provide new and easy ways of doing hard manual work and be more economical. At first there had been problems in their introduction, which led to the Swing Riots, a widespread uprising in 1830. Agricultural workers in southern and eastern England protested at mechanisation and harsh working conditions that began with the destruction of horse-powered threshing machines. In time, the resistance to the new technology was overcome, with the advancement of technical development in most areas of life. John would often work with the blacksmith on the estate, who not only shoed the horses, but was already involved with the making of agricultural implements and had an interest in new developments.

Soon, it was time for John to decide on his future education; his interest in the new technologies and his ability in the sciences would decide the outcome. His father, Robert, would encourage him to go to one of the best universities and see that his costs were covered so he had a reasonable allowance.

Chapter 3
1848

The University of Cambridge is one of the most prestigious and oldest universities in the world. Founded in the year 1209, it is considered the fourth oldest university and has gained fame and respect the world over. It came into existence primarily because of an incident that took place in Oxford. The scholars at that time were not in favour with King Henry I, so when a woman was found dead in the city, two of the scholars of Oxford University (founded in approximately 1096) were suspected and given a death penalty. This event caused a great uproar in the city and the university started to protest, which caused a suspension. The scholars had to leave the city and move to Cambridge, where they founded a new institution to practice their knowledge. This institution was given the title of university by King Henry III in 1231.

Six young men who were enrolled at Trinity College in 1848 were introduced by their tutor and shown to their accommodation by the porter. Room 20 was occupied by Angus McDonald, William Brown and John Cromwell; in next door room 21 were George Armstrong, Frederick

Shawcroft and Peter Archer. They settled in and got to know each other and soon were great friends as they were all to study and live together.

At that time, all undergraduates would study for a Bachelor of Arts degree in both arts and science. From the time of Isaac Newton until the mid-nineteenth century, the university maintained an especially strong emphasis on applied mathematics and physics. The exam which the six young men would study to pass in maths and physics was known as a Tripos. This was the early days of technology, which would eventually lead to engineering courses. Cambridge in the 1830s was a time in which science was becoming increasingly important and was home to a group of scholars known as the 'Cambridge Network'. Three of these men were of particular importance: Charles Babbage and William Whewell were building the 'Difference engine' at this time, a mechanical precursor of the digital computer. Robert Willis was interested in applied mechanics and developed the 'Odontograph', a device to allow a craftsman to determine the proper shape of teeth on wheels of different diameters.

The students were taught by these scholars, which started their increased interest in technology. Angus would study the use of mechanics in the mining and textile industry; George became interested in steam engines. The study of strength of materials and bending moments used in bridge-building was the interest of Will. Fred was fascinated by naval architecture, and Peter continued his interest in Aeronautics. John linked his studies to agricultural machines. All these subjects were secondary to their main areas of study.

The students would meet up for meals and discuss their various interests, including sports and pastimes. They were able to carry on fencing and would test each other's ability, which helped to keep them fit. Football was popular; however, the rules were not clear, as each public school they had come from had different rules. This led to one Charles Malden getting together two men from each of the schools and two others, making fourteen in all, and meeting to form a common set of rules. So men from Rugby, Eton, Harrow, Winchester and other schools wrote down, after much discussion, what came to be known as the 'Cambridge Rules'. These set of eleven rules which everyone could agree upon were nailed to the trees surrounding Parkers Piece. This was the first time that football as we know it had formalised laws; it was the catalyst which spread the game to encompass every corner of the world.

The 'Mechanics', as the six were nicknamed by other students, all enjoyed playing football to the new rules and became part of the college team. The team would go on to win the first university cup and eventually play against other university teams.

The 'six' would often end up in the larger room 20, at first, to get to know each other; they would talk about their families and interests. At one such meeting, Fred, who was the dominant one and a born leader, said, "Come on, chaps, it's time we had a drink in the town."

"Right," said Angus, who was very persuasive and got the others to agree. They all ended up drinking in two of the local Ale Houses, the 'Eagle and Child', which got called the 'Eagle', and the 'Pickerel'. The 'Eagle' became their watering hole; it was preferred because it was where some of the local girls would be found, and there was often music and dancing. They would often be found having a break from their studies, although it was usually Fred and Angus who would go out drinking when the others would be working. Will did not go out as much as he was not keen on the girls, although he did make friends with a young stable hand who worked at the hostelry. George was concerned about becoming too familiar with the girls and said one evening, "You must all be careful not to get too involved with the girls; we do not want any trouble."

John said he agreed. "We can have a good time, but keep it from getting out of hand."

Fred and Angus were rather carefree, which led them into trouble. One evening they were drinking and making up to some local girls, which they often did, when Fred – who was handsome and loved the girls – sat Molly Good on his knee, which sparked anger in a group of local lads watching. Ned Sully, who was keen on Molly and was a bit of a bully, was the self-appointed leader of the group. He said, "Wait, lads; we will get them later and show them not to touch our girls."

The college gates were closed at ten thirty p.m., so Angus had made arrangements with the porter to wait for their return if they were late back. They left the 'Eagle' to return in time, saying their farewells to Molly and the girls. On passing a dark alley, they were set upon by Ned and his gang, and although they fought back well, they were outnumbered and left beaten up. Fortunately, they had no serious injuries, for when an alarm had been sounded and the police called, the thugs fled into the night. Fred and Angus were led back to their college, where the porter let them in, saying, "What a mess. Come on into my rooms and we will patch you up."

They told the police they were not sure who the lads were and they would not take the matter further. On returning to their rooms, the others were very concerned and upset at what had happened. Peter said, "Let's get some rest now and discuss it tomorrow after lectures."

The following evening, a meeting was held in room 20, where George was the first to speak. "We should teach these thugs a lesson they will not forget easily."

They all agreed. Angus said he knew who they were. "It was that bully Ned Sully who had led his pals on."

John said, "We will have to be careful not to be seen or we may end up falling foul of the law."

"Right," said Will. "We should wear masks when we attack and wait for them leaving the 'Eagle'. I will ask Tim the stable hand to let us know when they are leaving, and we should ask some other students to keep an eye out for the police."

All was arranged. Two nights later, Tim reported that Ned and six of his gang were in the ale house. They decided they could deal with them, so, masks on, they gathered around ten p.m. and it was not long before Tim reported that the gang were leaving and told them they would go down the rope works alley as a short cut. Three men waited at one end of the alley, the other three waited till the thugs, singing and laughing, entered the alley; then, on a single whistle, they attacked. The thugs stood no chance against men trained in unarmed combat, and soon Ned and his lads were on the ground with bruises and bleeding noses. Fred got hold of Ned and warned him that if ever any of them attacked a student again then they would end up wishing they were dead. A call came from the lookouts for them to disperse as the town watch was heading their way. They soon arrived back at the university, satisfied they had done a good job. When the watch came upon Ned and his gang, shocked and battered, they were surprised when Ned said, "Some masked men attacked us, but we don't know who they are." They were all too scared to say any more. The outcome of the encounter resulted in any groups of undesirables throughout the city being very careful who they approached. In fact, the 'Eagle' became a much happier place, without incident, the local lads enjoying a drink with the students. They would even sometimes play football together on a weekend, and some became good friends.

One lad, Billy Roper, was keen on rowing, and he said to the six students, "Why don't you come down one evening and have a go? It's good exercise, and you may enjoy being on the river."

John and Peter had done some rowing, and after some discussion they all went down to the boat club where Billy worked as a boat builder. There first experience of rowing as a team was rather poor, with Angus falling overboard. He came out with a red face, shouting, "Bloody silly boats; give me a horse any time."

They all had a good laugh and took Angus to dry out and have a drink. Soon, however, they became very efficient rowers as they were all fit young men.

The Boat Race is an annual set of rowing races between Oxford and Cambridge boat clubs, traditionally rowed between open-weight eights on the River Thames. The tradition was started in 1829 by Charles Merivale, a student at St John's College Cambridge and his old school friend from Harrow, Charles Wordsworth, who was studying at Christ Church Oxford.

The six students joined the boat club and received a hearty welcome. The annual race was to be held soon, when most of the Cambridge eight would retire, so the club was keen to have new rowers to pick a new team for 1850. George said, "We should form our own eight and appoint a cox."

"What a good idea," said John. "I know a very small student called Sid Cuthbertson who I will ask to be cox."

"Fine," said Fred. "I am sure we can find two strapping students at the boat club to join us."

So it was arranged, and the six became nine, who were often seen practising on the River Cam.

The boat race Championship Course has hosted the majority of the races. It covers a 4.2-mile stretch of the River Thames from Putney to Mortlake in West London. That year, 1849, the Cambridge light blue team were expected to win, for they were a seasoned team. As the boat club members and most of the students watched the event, the tide turned against the Oxford eight, who were leading. Both teams were neck and neck, with the crowd watching, screaming on their teams. The dark blue team from Oxford were soon overtaken by the stronger Cambridge team. A disappointment for the Oxford students, but a triumph for Cambridge, who won easily.

Cambridge needed a new team for the following year, so three teams were picked from the boat club members. One of the teams was the 'Mechanics' team, as it became known, and they had to compete with each other to be picked for the next boat race. Angus and the other mechanics now devoted a lot of time, after lectures, in improving their technique. They decided to only go out to the 'Eagle' once a week, their spare time after studies being divided between fencing, football and rowing.

One evening, after rowing practice, they met to talk things over in room 20. They had a few practice runs against the other teams, but were not always winning, so they were discussing what could be done. Fred, who was keen on boat building – his family were shipbuilders – said, "Why don't we design our own boat and get Billy to ask his company to build it?"

"Good idea," remarked Peter. "We could all contribute to the costs."

It was decided that Fred and Peter would draw up an improved sleek design, Will and George would search out lighter alloys for the fittings, and Angus and John would look for thinner but strong timber for the hull.

It took them some time to come up with the answers and an improved design. An arrangement was made after consulting Billy, when his company agreed on a price using the improved design and the new materials that the mechanics would supply.

Will and George found out about a Danish physicist named Hans Christian Ørsted, who had managed to collaborate with a German chemist, Friedrich Wöhler, to produce Aluminium in 1825. The most plentiful ore on earth, Alumina was difficult to extract and became more valuable than gold at first. It is very light, so Will and George found a supply, and after some experimentation found if they mixed Copper with the Aluminium it was still fairly ductile but much stronger. The alloy was later to be termed Duralumin when German metallurgist Alfred Wilm (1903) discovered it could be heat treated and when left at room temperature for several days would slowly harden. Will was able to consult his grandfather and was allowed to use the foundry to perfect an alloy casting that was light and strong. They set about producing any boat fittings required for the new 'shell'.

Angus and John had some trouble at first finding a source of low-density strong hull material; then, after some research, found a company that were starting to manufacture a thin composite called Plywood. This later would become known as Marine Grade Okoume Plywood, which was lighter than the conventional timber in use. Further, they found that Cypress was a good wood to use for the shell frame as it was light and withstood water damage. As time passed, the developments in Material Science expanded rapidly, and carbon-fibre-reinforced plastic would be the choice of the boat builders.

It took a few months before the material and parts were together. The construction went ahead rapidly. The new boat was approved and given the name 'Rapier', a fencing term but appropriate due to its sleek design and the connection with the owners. On launching, the builders and the students were all gathered to see the super shell perform. It was much lighter, and the mechanics team boarded and set off on the maiden trial. It proved a great success; as it moved gracefully and rapidly through the water, they all cheered and agreed on the performance, and then went for a drink to christen the boat.

Christmas was a time when the students returned home to their families, so arrangements were made to have a final race between the three teams in the new year

1850. The team to represent the university would then be selected.

The six returned to college in January, just in time to miss a terrible fortnight of high winds and heavy snow. They would have to wait for better weather to go rowing again. On meeting up in room 20, they got a fire going and settled down to talk about their homes and the various Christmas activities. Angus was telling them how he had met up with his fiancée Rose: they had gone together to the Presbyterian church, the national church of Scotland. Fred and Peter were Roman Catholics and told the group about their family gathering in church. John had met up with Grace and George with Caroline, and they both went to their local Church of England services at Christmas. Will said, "I have no interest in getting involved with girls", but had gone with his family to the local Methodist Church. This set off a big discussion about the need for Religion.

Fred was the one to say, "The Catholics are the true Christians."

The others could not agree with this. Will said, "In my mind, the non-conformists have the right way to worship."

Peter was the first to say, "I often have doubts about the truth, especially when you see the plight of some of the poor people and the terrible things that happen in the world."

They all said they had doubts, but in the end they came to an amicable agreement that Christ had lived and died to show the right path in life; that they should fight against evil and try where they could to help people to improve their lives. However you worshipped was not as important as making the right Christian decision.

After an horrendous January, February dawned bright, sunny and fairly warm for the time of year. A time was set and the three teams assembled to race down the Cam. The boats were lined up and the boat master used a musket to fire a shot to signal the start. All three boats got away well, the new shell leading as expected. Suddenly, the 'Rapier' slowed down, the other two boats surging on. Peter had got cramp and nearly lost his oar; however, he recovered quickly, not wanting to let the team down. Sid the cox was screaming, "Come on, we can catch them"; and so they did, but it was a near thing as they passed the other teams at the finish line to the delight of their fellow students watching.

There was a meeting in the boat club, and the selection committee awarded the mechanics team the honour of rowing for the university. The team were overjoyed and relieved that their hard work had brought success; they would now train to compete in the Boat Race.

Life continued at college; the six would always spend time building up knowledge of their chosen subjects, discussing their findings with their group and in tutorials. All were doing well in their academic work, and in any tests or exams George would often come out top, although the others were not far behind. The danger was

41

not to work too hard; the Mathematics and Physics degree was very demanding, so it was a relief to have activities such as rowing to turn to when they had free time.

The University of Cambridge light blue crew, the mechanics, were to be coached by the Thames waterman and world champion sculler Bob Coombes. However, the team were very disappointed, after much training and preparation, when the universities were unable to agree on a date for the race in both 1850 and 1851. It was said the main reason for this was that Oxford was not happy with Cambridge using watermen as Boat Race coaches. Oxford had prevented their use since 1841, but Cambridge would not do so until 1873. Bob was rather mad at this, and so as not to let all the hard work go to waste, he managed to arrange a race with the Oxford coach Thomas Egan, whom he knew well. It was an unofficial race, but both crews were delighted at the competition.

At the appointed time, the crews and their shells were assembled and made ready at the start on the Thames near Putney. Fred remarked, "It's a fine day, just right for rowing."

Sid the cox agreed as they climbed into 'Rapier'. All the rowers were ready and eager to go as the starting shot rang out. The students and staff from both universities who had turned up cheered their sides on; some ran or cycled along the embankment. Both crews rowed steadily until after about two miles the 'Rapier' proved its worth and with the Cambridge crew egged on by Sid, they made an extra effort and surged ahead. By the time they reached Mortlake, they were at least ten lengths ahead and won the race easily. The Oxford crew said it was a remarkable victory, Thomas Egan remarking that they would have to consider a new boat design.

After getting their boats ready for the return journey to their respective boat houses, all the crew members of both shells were invited to dinner, paid for by Bob, who had put a large bet on Cambridge to win.

After their victory, the six had less time to devote to rowing and allowed their shell 'Rapier' to be used by the club as they desired. Their main aim now was to pass their final exams, so they would keep up their fencing practice, football at the weekend and occasionally go rowing.

1851 was the year they took their final exams and became twenty-one years old. Fred had said, "We should celebrate each of our birthdays at the 'Eagle' and have a big party after graduation."

John said, "You could all come to Longmeadows. I could arrange a dance and we could ride and hunt together."

"That is a jolly good idea," said Peter. "From there we could then head home."

It was agreed as something to look forward to. The final exams were over by the end of June. Each student handed in a thesis based upon research of their chosen topic: Angus had based his work on using steel props for mining, George had worked on a steam engine to power a land vehicle, Will had put forward a new steel bridge design. Fred worked on a revolutionary ship design with a riveted steel structure; Peter was fascinated with flight: his work was a method to improve lift during take-off and landing control. John had worked on a new harvesting machine. A time of waiting now started before the results were announced. The mechanics returned home for the summer, each to work in their family business. Before they all headed off, they did have a night out to celebrate John's birthday on 2nd July.

"Now we are all twenty-one, we can decide our own futures," said Angus.

They all agreed it was a tradition to become an adult at the age of consent, as it was called. "We are now men of Cambridge."

Chapter 4
1852

It was a time of adjustment for the friends; they had all missed the comradeship and companionship of like minds and to experience new challenges.

Angus was helping in his father's companies and was quite happy at first to be home. He loved his family and would see Rose on a regular basis, but always felt he should be developing new ideas for the mining industry. Rose could see he was not really content, so when he said, "I love you very much but think we should wait to get married", she was not surprised.

George worked at his family engineering company, which specialised in the manufacture of steam boilers. He enjoyed the experience at first, although his real interest was steam engines. He would meet Caroline and they became more romantically involved. When she came to stay with his sisters, she would discreetly steal into his room, where they would make intimate love. They had to be very careful, as his parents were quite strict about sex before marriage. He did say, "If you could wait a while, I will marry you."

"But you must," said Caroline. "What if I become pregnant?"

"All right, my love, I will ask your father for your hand in marriage and we will get engaged," replied George.

Will had many friends, some of whom were his three sisters' friends, and a group would gather at Bridge Manor at the weekend. Will, although a good-looking man, never got too involved with anyone. He spent time working at the foundry with his grandfather, enjoyed his sports and kept up his interest in bridge building.

Fred was very happy working at the shipyard and studying naval architecture with his father's experienced staff. He would often wonder what else he could get involved with as he had gained an interest in working with metal. His company was building modern wooden clippers. Peter was invited to work with Fred, but his interest took him to work with John Stringfellow, who employed him to help with his early flying machine. Peter would also help his father with the horses. Both Peter and Fred were good horsemen and would go riding with other friends from the village. Peter and Jane Moore had become romantically involved. Fred, who had plenty of admirers, was very friendly with a number of young ladies without committing himself to any. They were not ready to make any long-term decisions.

John was now working with his father helping to run the estate and often ending up at the Croft farm, where the attraction was Grace. He said to Grace, "I will marry you as soon as I know what my future will be. I am not content and need to consider any options."

Grace replied, "Don't worry, I am not involved with anyone else. When you are ready, I will be waiting for you, my love."

John was still working on ideas for agricultural machines, as the farms on the estate covered a large acreage. Men were leaving labouring on farms to work for more money in the industrial towns and cities. There was a need for less labour-intensive methods of farming. John could see the need for more modern ideas, but, unfortunately, his father was not so sure and needed a lot of persuasion to change. The family had agreed to have the friends to stay at Longmeadows after their Graduation.

The friends all received confirmation by post that they had been admitted to the degree of BA in Mathematics and Physical Science. The ceremony was to take place on 30th June.

They had all decided to travel by horseback down to Cambridge, which for Angus and George was a few days' travelling. It meant they would have their own horses when they went on to Longmeadows. Fortunately, it was a good summer, which meant travelling was easy.

On arrival back at Cambridge, each Graduate was directed to the main hall of his college, where their academic gowns were waiting for them. Once all the men were gathered together, they would then process to the Senate House. The Senate House, which is situated in the centre of the city between King's and Gonville and Caius colleges, is built in the neo-classical style using Portland stone. The friends were concerned because it was nearly time to leave and Angus was missing. He arrived with only minutes to spare rather flushed and sweating with having to hurry. He had stopped to help a young lady in a carriage that had broken an axle; she was also heading to the ceremony, so he had given her a lift. It turned out she was the college principal's daughter. They all cheered at his arrival and set off to the Senate House, where the Graduates were presented college by college in order of foundation or recognition by the university. Each individual student was presented with his degree certificate by the Chancellor, which, in this case, was the Prince Consort, Prince Albert. It was a great honour for them to remember.

Most of the friends had family attending the ceremony who had journeyed down and stayed in Cambridge for the occasion. After the ceremony, the Graduates headed back to their colleges, where they had a light lunch laid on and met up with their families and tutors to be congratulated on becoming part of the elite Alumni.

After saying their farewells, the friends met at the stables and collected their horses for the ride to Longmeadows. They stopped at a coaching house overnight in London on the way down to break the journey and take it easy on man and horse. The six young gentlemen were treated well, especially as they had the coin of the realm. A celebration took place in the bar, which resulted in Angus and Fred in particular being rather worse for wear and had to be helped to bed. The landlord didn't mind when he was told they had recently graduated from Cambridge. In the morning, he made sure they had a full English breakfast and provided them with a packed lunch to have on the way. Although, as they set off, they had to contend with rain steadily falling for the first hour or so, by lunch time just outside Sevenoaks it cleared and was followed by hot sunshine which soon dried them out. "Typical English weather," said Angus.

"It's not like this in Scotland, then?" replied George.

"No, it's much better in the lowlands," said Angus with a grin.

"Don't kid yourself, you hairy ginger daydreamer," uttered Fred, and at that they all had a good laugh at Angus's expense. Even though they had rain, the ground was fairly hard and they made good progress to arrive at Longmeadows near Midhurst around teatime.

They were made most welcome by John's family and congratulated on their awards. After settling their horses, they had tea and cake, before being shown to the bedrooms they would stay in. John's sister, June, led them to their rooms, saying, "If you need anything, just ring for the maid."

Fred was really taken with June, as she was a beautiful young lady who was now twenty-three years old and unmarried. Fred was quick to ask June, "Have you a suitor or young gentleman wanting your hand?"

June said, "I have had a number of offers; however, I have not found the right man yet. I am not in any hurry."

That night, much conversation and fun was had over dinner. Fred and June seemed to have much in common and spent time with each other when the meal was over. John remarked after June and her parents had retired, "You seem to be taken with my sister."

George was the first to say, "He's taken with all pretty women!"

"She is a lovely woman with a good brain. I really like her," was Fred's reply.

The next two days were spent riding or hunting on the South Downs or on their return practising their fencing skills and other sports. They played tennis with June and her friends and even tried playing croquet on the lawn.

On one occasion whilst hunting for deer in the forest a few miles from the house, they came across other tracks. Angus immediately recognised them and called out to the others, "Those are wild boar tracks."

"Yes," said John, "you are right, there are some in this area. Shall we try to catch one?"

"Come on," said George.

Will said, "Let's follow them."

They followed the tracks deeper into the forest. Peter, who was in the lead, managed to see one as it was about to enter a group of dense bushes, and he immediately shot it from his horse – a brilliant shot. Fred, who was just behind him, jumped off his horse to examine it, and at that precise moment a large male boar with great tusks charged at Fred. To his relief, as he drew his knife to defend himself, two shots rang out from John and George, killing the beast. It was within a foot of reaching Fred, who thanked his friends: "I will never forget that you saved me from injury."

"Come on, we had better load up these beasties," said Angus.

"Yes," said Will, "and get back to cook them for dinner. I love roast boar."

With much merriment they all agreed, then loaded up the kill, mounted and headed back to the house.

Back at the house, the servants, under the command of Mrs Briars the cook, unloaded the boars from the horses of John and Peter and took them to the kitchen to prepare them for the evening meal.

That evening after dinner, the friends were deep in conversation discussing their future, and they all admitted they were not completely happy with their present situations. It was then that Fred said, "I am seriously considering joining a cavalry regiment."

Angus replied, "All our fathers were cavalry officers; why don't we follow them and spend a few years serving our Queen and country?"

"I am not sure my parents would want to pay for a commission after Cambridge," answered Will.

"I think it's a good idea," said John. "Why don't we join as troopers and work our way up?"

Peter said, "I am all for a change before I settle down."

George said, "We might even see more of the world – but it could be dangerous."

"Come on," replied Fred, "that's part of the challenge as a cavalryman. We can all ride and fence well, and we will be trained in any case."

It was settled they would sort out a regiment. "I favour heavy cavalry," said Angus.

"No," said John, "we should join a light cavalry regiment."

Light cavalry played a key role in mounted scouting, escorting and skirmishing; while lacking the offensive power of heavy cavalry, they were extremely effective against unprepared infantry, cavalry and artillery. They were used to press a victor's advantage or to screen retreating forces from further attack. No armour was worn, so they were light and fast in a charge. They usually carried a carbine, a sabre and, in some cases, a lance.

Heavy cavalry was a class of cavalry intended to deliver a battlefield charge and to act as a tactical reserve, often termed 'shock cavalry'. They were generally mounted on large, powerful warhorses and often wore armour and carried a heavy sword and a lance.

All the friends agreed they would join the same regiment together, and a safer option would be the light cavalry. After much consideration, they decided that to be fair and prevent any bad feelings when they told their families, they would select a new regiment. They listed the various regiments of Dragoons, Lancers and Hussars, and Peter picked out the 11th Hussars. "They are a good, well-respected regiment."

"Yes," said George. "They have recently been re-formed as Prince Albert's Own."

"I will write immediately to their headquarters in Winchester," said Fred. "We will ask if we can enrol as troopers."

They were all in accord and happy with their choice; now they would have to return home and face their families.

In 1840, the 11th Hussars was named Prince Albert's Own after Queen Victoria's consort, who became 'colonel of the regiment'. Prince Albert's interests included military tactics and equipment, and he helped design a new uniform for the regiment. Purely by coincidence, this included cherry- or crimson-coloured trousers, unique among British regiments and worn ever since. They were named 'Cherrypickers'. This nickname had been acquired during the Peninsular War, when a troop of the 11th Hussars had been forced to hide in cherry trees to avoid the French.

Their decision made, the friends told John's parents what they were planning. The ladies were against the idea, and June said, "But you might be sent to war and be hurt."

"Nonsense," said Robert Cromwell. "It will be good for them and widen their experience on active service for their country."

"They have spent all that time getting a good education; why waste it?" replied Alice.

"It won't be wasted," said Robert. "I did a similar thing at their age; it will make them better men. They can come back to their Engineering when they return."

The rest of the evening was taken up with packing for the five returning home. John was relieved that in the end his parents had accepted that they were joining the Army.

Fred and June had become very close. They were opposites in temperament, he being rather carefree and her having much more common sense; however, they had loved being together. Before turning in, Fred had invited June to walk out into the garden. He said to her, "I have really enjoyed your company; would you like to come west to stay with us in Chard House? I would love you to come."

"I would be very happy to see you again, as I have grown very fond of you."

So it was arranged: the following weekend, Fred would return for June and she would have a few days' holiday with the Shawcrofts.

The following morning, John and June said farewell to their friends and the friends all thanked the Cromwells for their hospitality. Fred said, "I will let you all know when I receive a reply from the Hussars."

"Best of luck to you all on your return home," remarked John.

Angus and George had a long journey ahead of them and headed north together, saying goodbye to Fred, Peter and Will, who would start west together. They would part after reaching Andover and Will would go northwest, heading for Ironbridge.

Fred and Peter reached Chard House in time to settle in and change for dinner. Edward Shawcroft had invited Peter's parents to dinner to welcome them back as a celebration of their achievements. During the conversation, Fred announced their plan to join the cavalry and that he had invited June Cromwell over to stay. The ladies present were not pleased with the idea; however, the men thought it a good thing to do before they settled down. Edward said, "I could get you both a commission in my old regiment."

Peter helped by saying, "We decided as a group of friends to join together in a new regiment and to earn any promotion as a better option"

Edward and Jack Archer both gave their approval. "We are proud of your decision," said Edward, and Jack agreed.

Will arrived home late that night when most of the household were in bed. He handed his horse to the stable boy, who was aroused from his sleep with instructions to look after Will's horse, which was tired and hungry after a long ride. Will managed to help himself to a meal before going upstairs to his room. His sister, April, heard a noise on the stairs – she was an avid reader and was still reading.

On seeing Will, she gave him a hug, saying, "How happy I am to see you back; we do miss you."

"And I you. Now get to sleep," replied Will.

It was a few days before Samuel Brown was home again from London, so Will waited until an appropriate moment over dinner to tell his family what he had decided. His mother said, "You should do as you feel, so as not to say, when you are too old, 'I wish I had taken the chance when I had it'."

His father was pleased he was applying to join the 11th Hussars. "It will be a good experience for you; they are one of the best cavalry regiments. I will contact the regiment and tell them about you and your friends."

George and Angus had stopped for lunch at a hotel named 'The Victoria Arms' in a village called Towcester. At first, they were looked at with some suspicion; however, once the landlord saw they were young gentlemen and had the means to pay, they were made very welcome. After they and their horses were fed and watered, they rode on until it was getting dark. Angus said, "We must find somewhere to stay the night."

"Yes," replied George. "My backside has gone numb. We should not be far from Nottingham."

A Coaching Inn was found on the way into the city, where they were provided with a welcome bed and sustenance for man and beast. The next morning, they were up and away early and managed to reach Belsay

Hall late in the evening, just in time for dinner. The Armstrong family was delighted to see them. After introductions and some hugs and kisses, Mary Armstrong instructed the housekeeper to prepare a room for Angus. "I am very glad of the offer to stay," said Angus.

"That's fine," replied Mary. "You are most welcome. Now freshen up, then come down for dinner."

Henry was pleased when they explained their plan to join the Army. "You should enjoy the experience, although it's not all fun; it will be hard work at first."

"Don't forget, you might be put in dangerous positions," said Mary. "But if that's what you want, go for it."

George replied, "We want to follow in our fathers' footsteps before we are too old." He was rather pleased with the outcome and enjoyed the rest of the evening with his family.

The next morning, with horse and rider refreshed, Angus said, "Goodbye, and thank you for your hospitality. George, I will be in touch as soon as we know the outcome of our application."

"Farewell and God's speed," said Henry.

Then off Angus galloped towards Scotland. He still had a long ride ahead of him, but made good progress in brilliant weather, stopping overnight at an inn he knew in Coldstream. By the time he got there it was late; however, he was made welcome and provided with accommodation and stabling. Eager to reach Ormiston, he was off at the crack of dawn and arrived home at lunch time, to be greeted by his sisters Ann and Ruth and Jean, his mother. Fergus, his father, was working at the textile mill, so Angus said nothing about his future plan to join the army.

Once lunch was over and information exchanged, Angus said, "I will ride over to Tranent House to see Rose and bring her back for dinner. Is that all right, Mother?"

"Of course," said Jean. "She has been over often to see us while you were away; but get yourself cleaned up and changed."

Rose was delighted to see Angus; she was in the garden and saw him coming. As soon as he dismounted, she was in his arms and they embraced. "Tell your mother you are coming to our house for dinner," said Angus, "so get ready for the ride."

They entered the house, where Rose got ready, while Angus was greeted by her family. On the ride back to Ormiston, Angus told Rose, "I have decided to join my friends and join the Army when our application is approved."

Rose replied, "I thought you were home for good now and we could marry."

"We can still get married," remarked Angus, "but I am not sure when."

"Can you remember what happened the last time you were home? I am sure I am with child."

They stopped and kissed. Angus was a little shocked, but overcome with emotion and love at the same time.

"We will need to arrange our marriage as soon as possible before I am called away," said Angus. "I do love you, Rose."

"I love you, too, and look forward to being a wife and mother."

That evening over dinner, Angus told his family his plans to join the cavalry and to marry Rose. They were not too happy about him going to join an English regiment, and Fergus said, "I do not mind you joining the cavalry, but why not a Scottish regiment, laddie?"

"I formed a great bond with my Cambridge friends; we are all joining together and decided it was the best solution to join a different new regiment, Prince Albert's Own."

It was finally settled: Angus and Rose would marry and Angus would become a trooper.

Fred returned to Longmeadows in a family carriage driven by a stable groom called Harry, who Fred and Peter had grown up with. When he arrived, June was already packed and ready to go. However, he was ready for some refreshments and a little rest, and so were the horses and Harry. He was greeted by John and the family. "Have you heard any news?" said John.

"Yes, but just to say they had received our request and would consider us for their next intake, which would be in September," replied Fred. "I will inform the others when I get back home."

An hour later, they were driving back to Somerset, getting to know each other better. June said, "I would like to do something with my life instead of just being a secretary for my father."

"I can understand that; it's not easy for a young lady, and that is why we are interested in having the experience of serving our country."

By the time they reached Chard House, they both knew they were right for each other. As they entered the house, leaving Harry to see to the luggage and the horses, Fred whispered to June, "I think I love you."

She said, "I might get used to hearing you say that."

They were then greeted by the Shawcroft and Archer families, who welcomed June to their home and introduced her to each person. That evening, they had a splendid dinner, with the main course being venison caught in the grounds, followed by a wonderful ice cream and fruit dish. At the end of the evening, June said, "I feel most welcome; it is just like home. Thank you for a lovely evening."

The next morning, it was a lovely summer day. Fred and June rode out on to the Downs, enjoying the company of each other. After racing back to the house, they were hot and sweaty and decided to have a swim in the lake on the estate. Both could swim well, and they found a secluded spot. "Don't look while I disrobe," said June. "I will go behind that bush and get undressed. See you in there."

Once in the water, they swam and splashed, which eventually led to a kiss and a full embrace. It was inevitable that it led to them making love, as they were by then both eager to have each other abandoning themselves to pleasure. The next day, Fred, who was very much in love, took June into the garden, where he knelt before her and said, "Will you marry me?"

"You are the man I have been waiting for; of course I will! I love you."

"We will go into town and I will buy you an engagement ring," said Fred. "We will arrange the marriage when I know my future."

The family were told at dinner and were very happy to congratulate them.

June returned to Longmeadows with Fred and they informed the Cromwells, who were surprised at the speed of the engagement, but at the same time delighted their daughter had found a suitable young gentleman. John was a little sceptical and said to Fred, "Knowing you, are you sure you want my sister and you won't disappoint her?"

"John, I love her. She is the one for me. Can't you see that?"

"Yes," said John. 'I just wanted to be sure."

Fred had to return home to work, saying farewell to the family and promising June he would be over to see her whenever he could.

A period began when each of the friends went back to their work, waiting for news from Fred. A month later, a letter arrived from the 11th Hussars. It read:

Further to your request to join this regiment, we have received a recommendation from a senior staff officer, High Command, who has explained who you are and recommended your enlistment. We feel as you are sons of officers of high standing who served at Waterloo, you should be enrolled as junior officers. However, we understand your wishes to begin as troopers, which will give you an insight into the life of the rank and file and if found suitable to become officers. We would therefore request that you make your way to the Upper Barracks, Winchester, for initial training in time to start on Monday 1st September. Please reply to confirm your time of arrival and commitment to the service.

Further, please do not bring your own horses; you will be provided with regimental horses from our stables. Once enlisted, you will receive uniform and equipment from our Quartermaster Sergeant.

Yours sincerely
Major C. A. Beaumont
Training Commandant

After the letter arrived, Fred immediately sent a message to Angus, George, and Will. He called to see Peter and would ride over to see John and June. They were all to gather at Chard House by coach in time to get down to Winchester on the Sunday. Fred advised them to bring all necessary personal items for a long stay.

Chapter 5
1853

A letter was sent from Angus thanking Fred for the much-awaited information and asking if Fred, Peter and their young ladies could come up to Ormiston for his wedding. A similar letter was sent to the other friends. The wedding would take place a fortnight before they would leave for enlistment. Angus said they could all stay at Ormiston Hall and could they arrive the day before the wedding or sooner? All would be prepared for a two-night stay.

All of the friends were amazed at the news of the wedding; they would not miss seeing Angus married. They all travelled to Ormiston and arrived the day before the wedding. George managed to bring Caroline, Peter invited Jane, John brought Grace, Fred and June came with them and Will came with his sister April. When they had all arrived, Angus greeted them, saying, "How pleased I am you have all managed to get here. You have met my family. I will show you to your rooms so the men can get ready for my stag party. The ladies will dine with my family."

A room had been booked at 'The George' in Edinburgh, and a family coach took the friends to the hotel. They had a delicious meal followed by drinks, they played billiards and darts and had a jolly good evening. On the way back, they sang some bawdy songs, and most of them were in a nearly drunken state.

Angus, sitting next to Fred, told him, "I could not go off to the Army without marrying Rose, for obvious reasons. I do love her."

"I am sure you do; she is a lovely lassie, as you Scots say," Fred replied.

"Aye, she is at that. I want you as my best man."

At Tranent House, they had been preparing for weeks for the wedding of Rose to Angus. The wedding would take place at the local Parish Church, followed by a reception at the house and grounds. A large marquee was erected on the main front lawn. The ceremony was a wonderful affair, with everyone in their best attire, the Scots in Scottish dress, showing off their tartans. Angus looked great – a true proud McDonald – and Rose was a beautiful bride, while Fred played his part well as the best man. Back at the house, the reception went ahead, and speeches were made after a lovely meal with plenty of drinking. Scottish dancing followed, with everyone joining in, even if they did not know how. There was only one problem: when Fred and George fell in the fountain, part-drunk, showing how good they could balance. A good time to be remembered by all.

Angus and Rose went off by carriage for a honeymoon in the Highlands near Oban. The rest of the company departed for home or would stay overnight and then depart. The friends other than Angus stayed overnight with their ladies at Ormiston Hall. Each departed the next day to return south: George and Caroline to Belsay; Will and April to Ironbridge; Fred, Peter and Jane to Chard; and John, Grace and June to Longmeadows.

It would only be a short time before the friends would report to Winchester and a different life. Angus could take his wife with him, but was not happy to do so because of the future birth of his first child. The other friends did not want to commit themselves to marriage at present until they were sure of their situation in the army. Fred had promised June they would marry in the spring of next year, "when we will have a good Catholic marriage and the best reception ever," he had told her.

The friends all arrived at different times to assemble at Chard House. To enable them to transport their luggage, those living in the south travelled by carriage, Angus and George by coach. Taking a large carriage provided by Fred's family, they made their way to the Hussars barracks in Winchester. They were introduced to the commanding officer and then led by a sergeant to their living accommodation, where they were lucky enough to be given a room together with four other new recruits, making ten troopers. Each troop of ten men was instructed by a sergeant. Will was the first to say, "Well, it's not like home."

"No," replied John, "but it is clean and we all have a good bed and a wardrobe."

After introducing themselves to the other four troopers, they were marched out by their troop leader, Sergeant Henry Brown, and taken to the company stores. There they were kitted out with their uniforms, carbine, sabre and dagger and told to get dressed as troopers, then to assemble on the parade ground to be taken to select their horses.

The horses were all of the Friesian breed or similar; for the light cavalry they were required to be light, fast, tough and of good agility. To look right for parade or escort duty, the regiment selected horses of the same colour; chestnut was selected by the 11th Hussars as the colour would blend in when scouting for enemy positions. The regimental stables were massive, with a separate wing for each cavalry troop. When the friends saw their horses, they were delighted at the beauty of the breed.

The sergeant took them to a horse in turn, then said, "You can name your own horse; he or she will be with you as long as you are in the service. However, you are also responsible for your horse's welfare. You will feed him and muck out after him; the horse will be your constant companion. Trained well, a good horse may help save your life."

Troopers were selected because they could ride a horse. The friends were all good riders; however, the demands in the cavalry were a lot different to riding for pleasure. The saddle in use was wood arched with flaps crafted to carry an approximate weight of 100kg. The shape of the saddle brought the cavalryman closer to the horse, allowing improved contact between the rider's legs and the flanks of the animal. Felt was fastened to the side-boards and a blanket was used, alleviating the heat and stress suffered by the horse.

Fred and the others soon got to know their horses. "I will call mine Bob," said Fred.

Angus replied, "Mine will be called Tartan."

Will picked Bolt, John decided on Storm, George called his Geordie and Peter said, "If John has picked Storm, mine is Lightning."

During the next six months, man and horse were trained together. They were taught to ride with bent knees with firm squeezing of the thighs to ensure a safe seat, particularly when they had to ride hands free. The use of the sabre was important; they would charge and slash at cabbages mounted on poles. They were trained to charge at other troops in mock battles using quick starts and stops and sharp turns or pirouettes, the most important skills to teach a cavalryman. To improve their skills using their carbines, they were expected to spend time every day on the shooting range. Self-defence techniques were part of the training, using a dagger or unarmed combat in case they were unhorsed. Riding procedures for combat and ceremonial use were a necessary part of the training. The six friends passed out with commendation as they were shown to be the best troop during the training course. The major was delighted with their achievements and recommended they complete officer training, for the regiment needed more good officers.

Before any officer training could take place, the regiment was commanded to send a company of two squadrons consisting of two hundred and fifty men and horses to India. At this time, the British Empire was the largest empire ever known, with colonies throughout the world, due mainly to the Navy being a dominant force at sea. This meant the army was stretched to its limits to keep its colonies safe.

The remaining troopers of two squadrons, which included the friends' troop, were to train to take part in the very first army manoeuvres in preparation for any future conflict. Although the troopers were released at Christmas for a short period, some stayed at the barracks because of the bad weather or because the food would be better than what would be available at home.

Fred said to the other friends, "You are all invited to Chard House, which is a manageable distance."

John said, "I can make it home; it's not too far to Longmeadows."

The others took up the invitation. All had a good Christmas, returning to the barracks after the celebrations.

In the spring, they were allowed leave before the manoeuvres took place. It was then that Fred had arranged his marriage to June. It was planned so that his friends could attend before their return to the regiment. June and her family had prepared the wedding to be held in the local Catholic church, with a reception in Longmeadows' great hall. The friends all turned up on their regimental horses in full dress uniform and formed a Guard of Honour after the wedding.

Angus was best man, he and the other troopers looking splendid in their uniforms as the vows were taken. The reception went well, with most of the friends rather worse for wear after the drinking and dancing was over, so they were encouraged to stay the night.

Fred and June had a few days together before he had to return. The others had to ride back to Winchester the following day.

The Chobham Common in Surrey was the site of the Great Camp, where the first army manoeuvres took place and where Queen Victoria reviewed her troops.

At this time, supply duties were the responsibility of the Commissariat (a uniformed civilian body, principally responsible for food, forage and fuel), while provision of arms, ammunition and other critical stores was the responsibility of the Board of Ordnance. They would eventually become the Royal Army Service Corp. Once they set up the tents and other necessary facilities, the troops were moved to the site. The two squadrons of the 11th Hussars, which included the friends, were camped next to the other Light Cavalry regiments. Also present were the Heavy Cavalry, the Infantry and the Artillery regiments who were stationed in the home country.

Before the start of the war games, each regiment was paraded before the Queen and her Consort. The Queen thanked the men on parade for their smart turn-out and said how proud she was of her army. She received three cheers from the gathered troops.

Many mock battles took place. The friends were provided with special blunt swords to attack artillery, who fired blanks, and infantry, who had to fire at the ground. Further, they charged other cavalry units, twisting and turning in hand-to-hand combat.

"This was good training for a real battle," Angus was heard to say on return to camp after a hectic encounter with a Heavy Cavalry squadron from the Life Guards.

"I have a few bruises here and there, but at least we did come out of it well," said Peter.

"The Colonel took me to one side and remarked upon how well we had done and that he needed more officers to lead his new troopers," reported Fred.

All the friends were now happy to be recommended for officer training. They had experienced at first hand the life of a cavalry trooper and would appreciate the better conditions that were provided to officers.

The friends were sent to the Royal Military College, which was later to become the Royal Military Academy at Sandhurst. To students who had already completed the initial training in their regiments, they could attend a short course providing them with the basic requirements of an officer. The course covered military planning, officer duties, line of command, tactics and decision-making on the battlefield. Mock battles were carried out and the study of troop field movements that could cause victory or defeat in battle. Their course ended with success for the friends, as the examination was easy for Cambridge graduates. At the passing-out ceremony, which was attended by their wives, girlfriends and parents, each student was presented with a special sword or sabre; the sabre being the weapon of choice for a cavalry officer. After the presentation, the friends and their families got together for a meal and a drink to celebrate their commissions to officers of the Queen.

On return to the barracks of the 11th Hussars, the six subaltern lieutenants were each to be given charge of a unit of new troopers as they were enlisted. The regiment was required to build up its strength, for there were rumours of a conflict starting in eastern Europe. So began an exhaustive few months of training, the sergeants taking each troop through their programme of hard battle tactics. Each of the lieutenants would join in, to see if they were competent and lead them in mock charges.

Angus was the first to say, "I am very pleased we became officers – the accommodation is much better!"

John said, "Meeting in the officers' mess is very pleasant as well."

Fred said, "I am pleased to see you are all content with your new roles."

Will remarked, "Do you know my troops are very keen to do well and because I have been through it like them, show me a lot of respect."

"We all feel the same, don't we," said George, and the others agreed it was correct.

Training continued at a pace, and the new troopers were soon showing signs of being an elite fighting force, taking pride in making their regiment the best. It was when Colonel Douglas was addressing the remains of the regiment that he announced news he had received from Army Command. The army was to prepare for hostilities: a war had broken out on the Crimean Peninsula and British troops were to be involved. "We have been commanded to be ready to form part of the Light Cavalry Brigade going overseas. You have trained well; I know I can rely on your bravery in battle."

Chapter 6
1854

The Crimean War was a military conflict fought from October 1853 to February 1856, in which Russia lost to an alliance made up of France, the Ottoman Empire, the United Kingdom and Sardinia. The immediate cause of the war involved the rights of Christian minorities in the Holy Land, then part of the Ottoman Empire. Longer-term causes involved the decline of the Ottoman Empire and the unwillingness of Britain and France to allow Russia to gain territory and power at the Ottoman Empire's expense. This led to a war that was said to stand out for its 'notoriously incompetent international butchery'. In October 1853, having obtained promises of support from France and Britain, the Ottomans declared war on Russia. They fought a strong defensive campaign and stopped the Russian advance at Silistra, in present-day Bulgaria. A separate action on the fort town of Kars in Western Armenia led to a siege, and a Turkish attempt to reinforce the garrison was destroyed by a Russian fleet at Sinop. Fearing an Ottoman collapse, the British and French fleets entered the Black Sea.

The regiment was directed to report at the Portsmouth docks to embark for the sail to the Black Sea. The evening before they were due to set off, the friends met in the officers' mess. Peter remarked, "I am excited that we will be seeing action, but at the same time a little afraid."

"Don't you worry about it, try to enjoy the experience of putting all your training to the test," Fred told him.

"We all feel some fear," said Angus. "However, you must show your men a bold front."

George concluded by saying, "Just think, we are going out of the barracks and abroad for the first time."

John said, "I am glad of the change. However, we should not drink too much before the journey tomorrow."

Will was quiet for a moment, before saying, "We should write to our families and let them know what is happening."

"Right," said Fred. "We've been so busy, I had forgotten about that. Let's all make sure we do that after the next drink."

The regiment of now two hundred and fifty men and horses, with the necessary ancillary equipment, assembled on the parade ground to ride off to the port of embarkation. A small contingent was to stay behind to look after the barracks. Once they arrived at the port, the task of loading the transport vessels began; each man was responsible for making sure his horse was tethered tightly and boxed into a compartment in the hold. Sea travel remained a highly stressful experience for the horses. The troopers loved their horses and made sure they were looked after.

The French, Sardinians, Ottomans and British landed at Eupatoria on 14th September 1854, intending to make a triumphant march to Sevastopol, the capital of the Crimea, with fifty thousand men. The thirty-five-mile traverse took a year of fighting against the Russians. Major battles along the way were Alma, Balaclava, Inkerman, Tchernaya, Redan and finally Malakoff.

The sea voyage to the Black Sea took a few weeks, so to troops used to land travel it caused some sea sickness with both men and horses. Angus, George and Will had the most sickness; the others came off lightly. When they reached the Mediterranean Sea, the weather calmed down, making the voyage more pleasurable; but on reaching the Black Sea, it became really sticky and hot. It was quite a relief when they landed at Calamita Bay. The Hussars disembarked, making sure the horses were in good fettle. Fred was heard to say, "I am sure the horses are as relieved as we are to be standing on firm ground again."

"Yes," said Peter, "they will be glad to munch at some fresh grass."

Due to the weather being so hot, the troopers were ordered to leave their fur-edged pelisse jackets behind on board ship; but this was regretted later when the temperature dropped. A gentle sea breeze off the sea refreshed the marching armies as they headed along the

Crimean Peninsula to within sight of Alma. Here, the river flowed into the sea just a few miles north of Sevastopol.

The uniforms of the British army were even more brilliant than they had been in 1815 at Waterloo. Decades of peacetime soldiering in England had left colonels with little to do but smarten up their uniform dress. The close-fitting, cherry-coloured uniform of the 11th Hussars, who now formed part of the Light Brigade, were but one example of the absurdities of military dress. The Brigade of Guards wore their unwieldy bearskins into battle for the last time in the Crimea. One of the Scots Guards was heard to say that his made a reasonable pillow for a night on the ground.

The first couple of nights the troopers had to sleep on the ground due to the fact that the British army had left its tents behind. The day after the landing, officers of the British Quartermaster General's Department foraged miles inland for waggons and baggage animals so they could transport the tents and equipment to the troops.

As they rested for the night before the battle of Alma, George settled down, saying, "I am glad it's still quite warm at night."

"That's a good thing," replied Angus. "The lack of food and water is more important; the men are suffering."

"Yes," said John, "someone has really cocked things up a bit."

"Come on, chaps, cheer up; have some of that lovely dried beef and a mouthful of water," were Fred's words to get them into a better mood. Surprisingly enough, they were so tired that most managed to sleep.

The next morning, the Battle of the Alma River took place. Russian commander Prince Alexander Sergeyevitch Menshikov rushed his available forces to the last natural defensive position before the city, Alma Heights, south of the Alma River. The allies made a number of disjointed attacks with their infantry divisions. The French turned the Russian flank with an attack up cliffs that the Russians had considered unscaleable. The British initially waited to see the outcome of the French attack; then, after two attempts, successfully assaulted the Russians' main position on the right. Eventually, superior British rifle fire forced the Russians to retreat. With both flanks turned, the Russian position collapsed and they fled. The lack of cavalry meant that little pursuit occurred. This was a mistake and would quickly lead to the re-formation of the Russian army. The 11th Hussars did not see action in the battle. After the battle, it was estimated that four thousand one hundred and three allied soldiers and five thousand Russian soldiers had been killed or wounded and would not fight again.

The six units commanded by Fred and his friends were ordered to carry out a reconnoitre of both sides of the road the army would take leading to Balaclava. As they approached an area near a valley north of the marching army, they came across a contingent of Russian cavalry heading to reinforce the Russian lines. From their position in the valley they could only see Angus and

Fred's troopers, who were leading over the brow of a hill. On seeing only the two units, they decided to attack them. The French were charging towards the Hussars and were surprised when an equal number of cavalry lined up on the hill. Fred took charge and ordered the whole complement of six units to be ready to attack the Russian cavalry. As he called out 'Charge', they headed down hill to meet the Russians with sabres unsheathed ready to fight. A bloody battle ensued, with a number of men on both sides being killed or wounded. However, the Hussars were far superior and soon a rout took place. The Russians were being slaughtered, so retreated.

"Let them go!" Angus called out, and the others agreed, so they made their way to the supply base, now set up to the southeast of Balaclava. They needed to see to the wounded – two troopers had been killed and six wounded. The friends had all fought bravely, with only slight cuts and bruises. That was their first taste of battle. After seeing the wounded were being cared for, they reported to the commanding officer. Before being attacked they had seen Russian troop movements heading towards Balaclava from the north; however, they estimated it would take several days for them to arrive.

The army marched on to the supply base, where they were happy to find that their tents and equipment had been set up. Some food and drink had also been transported to the base, which lifted the troopers' spirits.

John commented, "I am glad we can get fed tonight – I am starving."

Will replied, "It's getting colder, too."

"Yes," said Peter. "We had better find some blankets if we can."

"Pity our pelisse jackets have not been sent," remarked George.

"Come on," said Fred and Angus, "we have been ordered to the officers' mess tent."

At the mess, the six lieutenants were congratulated by Colonel Douglas for their bravery and fighting spirit. He remarked, "I have commended you all for your courage when attacked by a seasoned Russian troop. You and your men have proved your worth in your first engagement, so that all your hard training was rewarded."

Although they met only once during the Crimean War, Florence Nightingale and Mary Seacole are still remembered for the care and compassion they gave to the many wounded soldiers they would nurse.

Florence Nightingale, a white English social reformer, statistician and founder of modern nursing, came to prominence while serving as a manager and trainer of nurses during the Crimean War. She organised care for wounded soldiers at Constantinople, which gave nursing a favourable reputation, becoming an icon of Victorian culture, especially in the persona of 'The Lady with the Lamp', making rounds of wounded soldiers at night.

After some persuasion, the British Government funded Nightingale, who arrived at Selimiye Barracks in Scutari, which was on the Asiatic side of the Bosphorus, opposite Constantinople (Istanbul). This was three hundred and thirty-nine nautical miles away from the main British camp at Balaclava, which she never visited. Her team found that poor care for wounded soldiers was being delivered by overworked medical staff in the face of official indifference. Medicines were in short supply, hygiene was being neglected, and mass infections were common, many of them fatal. There was no equipment to process food for the patients. Florence sent a plea to *The Times* for a government solution to the poor condition of the facilities. The British Government commissioned Isambard Kingdom Brunel to design a prefabricated hospital that could be built in England and shipped to the Dardanelles. The result was Renkioi Hospital, a civilian facility that was under the management of Edmund Alexander Parkes. Renkioi had a death rate less than one tenth of that of Scutari.

Due to making improvements in hygiene herself, or by calling on the Sanitary Commission, Florence reduced the death rate from forty-two percent to two percent. During her first winter at Scutari, four thousand and seventy-seven soldiers died there. Ten times more soldiers died from illnesses such as typhus, typhoid, cholera and dysentery than from battle wounds. With overcrowding, defective sewers and lack of ventilation, the Sanitary Commission had to be sent out by the British Government almost six months after Florence arrived. They flushed out the sewers and improved ventilation.

Mary Seacole was a British Jamaican nurse, healer and businesswoman who set up the 'British Hotel' behind the lines during the Crimean War. She provided comfortable quarters for sick and convalescent officers; at the same time she provided succour for the wounded servicemen on the battlefield. Many were nursed back to health.

Mary relied on her skill and experience as a healer and a female doctor from Jamaica. Schools of nursing were only set up after the war, the first being the Florence Nightingale Training School in 1860 at St Thomas's Hospital in London. Mary was arguably the first Nurse Practitioner.

Hoping to assist with nursing the wounded on the outbreak of war, Mary applied to the War Office to be included amongst the nursing contingent, but was refused. She finally resolved to travel to the Crimea using her own resources to open the 'British Hotel'. Shortly afterwards, her Caribbean acquaintance, Thomas Day, arrived unexpectedly in London and the two formed a partnership. They assembled a stock of supplies and embarked on the Dutch screw steamer *Hollander* on its maiden voyage to Constantinople. On arrival, she transferred most of her stores to the transport ship *Albatross*, with the remainder following on the *Nonpareil*. It was a four-day voyage to reach the British bridgehead at Balaclava.

Lacking proper building materials, Mary built her hotel from salvaged driftwood, packing cases, iron sheets, and salvaged architectural items such as glass doors and window frames from the village of Kamara. Using local labour, the hotel was completed at a cost of £800. It included a building made of iron, containing a main room with counters and shelves and storage above an attached kitchen, two wooden sleeping huts, outhouses and an enclosed stable yard. Meals were served at the hotel, cooked by two black cooks, and the kitchen also provided outside catering.

Mary often went out to the troops selling her provisions near the British camp at Kadikoi and nursing casualties brought out from the trenches around Sevastopol or from the Tchernaya valley. She was a warm and successful physician, always in attendance near the battlefield to aid the wounded, and she earned many a poor fellow's blessing. She did all she could to bring comfort and alleviate suffering to the troops, giving freely to such as could not pay. She was widely known to the British Army as 'Mother Seacole'.

When the call went out through the local and national papers for young women to go out to help Florence Nightingale to nurse the soldiers out in the Crimea, two of the young ladies who answered the call were Ruth McDonald and April Brown.

Ruth McDonald, the sister of Angus, was a strong, lively girl, and unlike her sister Ann, was ready to help and was determined to become a nurse. Her father, Fergus, was proud of her decision, but her mother was very worried. "I don't want to lose a daughter as well as a son."

Ruth replied, "I am going out as a nurse, not into combat."

So, after much argument and refusals to help from some of her family, they at last gave their blessing. She was accepted by the Nightingale Commission and travelled down to the office in London.

April Brown, the sister of Will, was another determined young woman, tough and resilient from working in the family foundry business. Her thoughts were always with her brother, whom she loved, and because she had no other ties, her first reaction upon reading the paper was to help. She told her family, "I feel I must do something to help the boys out in the Crimea. I have decided to become a nurse and go out to help."

Her father, who was at home, was a Senior Staff Officer. He knew the problems to be overcome out in the war zone. "I believe you will find it quite hard and difficult to work with the many wounded soldiers, some who are dying in poor conditions. However, what you are doing is most honourable. I am proud of your decision – may God keep you safe."

April was also accepted by the Commission and without knowing of the decision Ruth had made, headed down to London at the same time.

Ruth arrived at the office in London after a journey by coach and cab to be greeted by a British Army doctor, who was also heading for the Nightingale Hospital. Dr

Paul Ransome was from Kendal, where he had grown up, and later in London, where he had studied medicine. He had been asked to take charge of ensuring the twelve young ladies selected as nurses were protected. Ruth and Paul were attracted to each other from this their first meeting. Ruth met some of the other nurses, then they were told to wait, as two more young ladies were due to arrive to complete the complement. When they walked into the room, Ruth and April looked at each other in astonishment, then realised who they were, their brothers' sisters. They hugged each other in greeting and from then on grew to be the best of friends.

They were taken by coaches to Portsmouth to be taken aboard a Royal Navy frigate, HMS *Bulwark*, to ensure their protection. Special cabins were provided for the ladies to enable them to have some privacy on the long journey. During the sea voyage, the nurses got to know each other well, particularly Ruth and April, who became very close friends. The nurses were invited to eat with the officers, which provided them with some enjoyable evenings. Often after dinner they would all take a stroll on deck. Ruth was often in the company of Paul. It was on one such occasion that he said, "I am growing very fond of you, Ruth. I just love your personality and your lovely voice."

"I am very much attracted to you; we get on well together."

At that they kissed – their relationship had started.

On their arrival at Constantinople there was little time for romance; the nurses arrived at the hospital at the same time as a ship-load of wounded soldiers. They were shown to their quarters in a side annexe of the hospital, where they were asked to change into new nurses' uniform and report for duty to help settle the newly arrived wounded. The conditions were far from good; however, they had to manage, although many of the nurses were horrified at the wounds some of the soldiers had received. Ruth and April were strong and worked hard helping the doctors and comforting the sick and wounded. At last worn out and shattered from their first introduction to the results of war, they were thanked by Florence, who said, "Thank you for joining our nursing staff and doing so well without much time to get to know the hospital. Go and get some rest; you will be up early in the morning when we will introduce you to your planned duties."

The Battle of Balaclava is remembered in the UK for the actions of two British units. At the start of the battle, a large body of Russian cavalry charged the 93rd Highlanders. Rather than form square, which was the traditional method of repelling cavalry, Sir Colin Campbell took the risky decision to have his Highlanders form a single line, two men deep. He had seen the effectiveness of the new Minié rifles with which the troops were armed at the Battle of Alma a month before. Being confident his men could beat back the Russians, the brave Highlanders were made ready for the Russian charge. They opened fire successively one line followed by the other as the cavalry charged towards them. In rapid time, one line would discharge their rounds, followed by the second line as the first line recharged ready to fire again. These tactics succeeded due to the steadfast Scots and the Minié rifle, forcing the Russian cavalry to retreat with many casualties. The Highlanders were seen as a 'thin red streak topped with steel', a phrase which became known as the 'Thin Red Line'.

The Minié rifle was an important infantry rifle of the mid-nineteenth century. A version was adopted in 1849 following the invention of the Minié ball in 1847 by the French Army captain Claude-Etienne Minié of the Chasseurs d'Orleans and Henry Gustave Delvigne. The bullet was designed to allow rapid muzzle loading of rifles and brought about the widespread use of the rifle as the main battlefield weapon for individual soldiers. Before this innovation, the smoothbore musket, commonly using the buck and ball, was the only practical field weapon. The large heavy bullet of the Minié rifle could cause devastating wounds. The rifle had a reasonable accuracy of five hundred and fifty metres and was equipped with sights for effective aiming. It had a rate of fire of two to three shots per minute, the first of a new generation of weapons.

Soon after the stand by the Highlanders, a Russian cavalry movement was countered by the Heavy Brigade, who charged and fought hand to hand until the Russians retreated. This caused a more widespread Russian retreat, including a number of their artillery units. When the local commanders failed to take advantage of the retreat, the senior commander, Lord Raglan, sent out orders to move up and prevent the withdrawal of naval guns from the recently captured redoubts on the heights above the valley. Raglan could see these guns from his position on a hill; however, down in the valley this view was obstructed, leaving the wrong guns in sight. The local commanders ignored the demands, leading to the British aide-de-camp, Captain Nolan, personally delivering the quickly written and confusing order to attack the artillery. When Lord Lucan questioned which guns the order referred to, Captain Nolan pointed to the first Russian battery he could see, saying, "There is your enemy, there are your guns." Due to his obstructed view, these were the wrong guns.

Lucan passed the order to the commander of the Light Brigade, the Earl of Cardigan, resulting in 'The Charge of the Light Brigade'. Under the command of the Earl of Cardigan, the Brigade consisted of the 4th and 13th Light Dragoons, the 17th Lancers and the 8th and 11th Hussars.

After a rather good sleep in their tents, the 11th Hussars were roused by a bugle call and told to assemble in front of their tents. The commanding officer, Colonel Douglas, told them. "Get your breakfast quickly. I want you to be ready for battle within the hour. The Russians are approaching at speed, and we need to be ready for action."

"Well," said Fred, "I had a feeling we would be in action today."

Peter replied, "I at least had a good sleep last night."

"Yes, I think we all did; better than sleeping on the ground, are you all agreed?" Angus remarked. The other friends said they felt much better for it.

"Come on, we need to get some food before it all goes," said John.

They quickly had breakfast – porridge and tea – then George went off to make sure the horses were fed and watered. The troopers in each unit were ordered by their officers to saddle up and prepare their horses, then to mount up as soon as possible. Soon, they could hear the sound of battle, as first the Highlanders, then the Heavy Brigade fought off the Russians. By then the whole of the Light Brigade were assembled ready for action at the mouth of the valley. The order was given for them to charge the batteries at the end of the valley, but the Light Regiments were unaware that they were the wrong target.

The Light Brigade set off down the valley with Cardigan in front leading the 11th Hussars in the charge on his horse Ronald. Almost at once, Nolan rushed across the front in an attempt to stop and turn the Brigade, which was aimed at the wrong target. Unfortunately, he was hit by an artillery shell and killed instantly, while the cavalry continued on its course into the valley of death.

The Brigade advanced down a gradual descent of more than three-quarters of a mile, one regiment behind the other, starting at a trot, then, when all hell broke out, at full gallop. Batteries were vomiting forth shells and shot, round and grape, one battery on the right flank and another on the left, with all the intermediate ground covered by Russian riflemen. As the Light Brigade approached within fifty yards of the end of the valley, where the mouths of the artillery had been hurling destruction upon them, they were surrounded and encircled by a blaze of fire.

As they ascended the hill at the end of the valley, the oblique fire of the artillery poured upon them from all sides. Many men and horses perished or were wounded. Angus and John were unhurt during the charge, but all the others had been wounded. They nevertheless continued and entered and went through the battery, the two leading regiments cutting down a great number of Russian gunners. Once they were past the battery, they then had to fight hand to hand against a mass of Russian cavalry. The following two regiments of cavalry continued the duty of cutting down the Russian gunners. Then came the third regiment, which endeavoured to complete the duty assigned to the Brigade. This body of men, composed of only six hundred and seventy men, succeeded in passing through the mass of Russian cavalry, believed to be five thousand two hundred and forty strong. Having broken through, the fighting hand to hand was horrific. Fred, who was injured in the leg by a shot, was holding his own, but he saw Peter about to be beheaded by a Russian and managed to stop his blade to give Peter a chance to thrust his sword into the man's heart. Angus and John had cuts to their arms and legs. Will was in the thick of it; he was caught by the edge of an enemy sword cutting across his chest, but swerved and removed the man's arm.

George was also fighting hard and received a cut to his shoulder. The bugle call sounded 'threes about', which was an order to charge back the way they had come, doing as much execution as they could on their return.

Lucan and his troops of the Heavy Brigade had entered the mouth of the valley, but saw no point in sacrificing more men to be mown down by the gun batteries. They were best positioned to render assistance to the survivors returning from the charge. The French Light Cavalry was more effective by clearing the Fedyukhin Heights of two half-batteries of guns, two infantry battalions and Cossacks to ensure that the Light Brigade would not be hit by fire from the flanks. Further, it provided cover as the remaining elements withdrew.

The aim of any cavalry charge is to scatter the enemy lines and frighten them off the battlefield. The bravery and courage of the Light Brigade so unnerved the Russian cavalry, which had been routed by the Heavy Brigade, that the Russians were set to full-scale flight. The shortage of men led to the failure of the British and French to follow up on the Battle of Balaclava, which led to a much bloodier battle, the Battle of Inkerman. The Russians attempted to raise the siege at Sevastopol with an attack against the allies, which resulted in an allied victory. This ultimately led to a total victory and the Treaty of Paris, when all hostilities ended on 30th March 1856.

The 11th Hussars had lost thirty troopers killed and the rest were wounded; the Light Brigade as a whole was decimated. In total at the end of the war, the number of men killed in action, died of wounds or died of disease on the allied side was 223,513. On the Russian side the number was 530,000, a terrible loss of life to prevent territorial gain.

All the friends were injured by gunfire and blade in the hand to hand fighting. They all managed to charge back, in retreat from the valley of death. Fred, looking back, saw one of his troopers unhorsed as the animal was hit by shellfire, and his instinct was to rescue him. Riding back under fire, he collected the trooper and got him to safety. He did this twice to rescue a second comrade, this time an officer from the Lancers. For his outstanding bravery under fire he was later awarded the Victoria Cross. All the members of the Light Brigade deserved a medal for their outstanding courage. On return to Britain, they all received a special medal.

Those who survived were helped by the Heavy Brigade to be transported back to the base camp, as best they could, using their own horses. Some of the Light Brigade still had their horses – somehow they had survived – although many were wounded, so they managed to ride back to the casualty station. As the friends assembled at the medical tent, they were really shattered from their brutal encounter. As they sat waiting for their wounds to be dressed, Angus was the first to say, "My friends, that was hell."

"What a mess up to lead us into that," said Peter.

John remarked, "Many of our regiment were killed. I saw Colonel Douglas take a direct hit head-on from a shell."

"Yes, what a waste," replied George. "I think the war is over for us."

The medics carried out emergency work such as stitching wounds and, where possible, removing shot and shrapnel. Once the troopers' wounds were dressed, they were crowded on waggons to be driven to the port for the crossing to Constantinople and the hospital at Scutari. Unfortunately, some died of their wounds before they reached the hospital; others had infectious wounds on arrival. Fred and the others made the journey successfully.

Ruth and April had been working hard with Florence and the rest of the nursing staff to make the hospital more sanitary, making sure hands were washed at regular intervals and after each contact with a soldier's wounds. Further, they were now isolating those men who had any disease that could be contagious, so as to contain the spread any further. Dr Paul and Ruth had become much closer, spending time working together and, when they had a spare moment, taking a break from the sick and wounded. It was one such break that Paul said to Ruth, "I do love you. When we return to England, will you marry me?"

Ruth replied, "I know you love me as I love you, and maybe I will marry you if you feel the same then. Let's wait and see."

Florence told the staff, "A rider has arrived from the port with news of the Battle of Balaclava. He forewarned us of the imminent arrival of a new intake of wounded soldiers from the battle. Although the Russians have been defeated, many of our men were killed or wounded. Let us prepare a new area with food and drink to welcome them. To work!"

The few troopers left to be cared for, including the six officers of the 11th Hussars, were given rough camp beds to rest and sleep on. "A doctor will look at your wounds in turn," a young nurse told them, as she and other nurses helped them to their beds.

As they came to see the wounds Angus had received, he gave a shout of surprise. "How in heaven's name did you get here, Ruth? Look," he shouted to the others, "it's my sister Ruth."

They were all astonished to see her. "Not only me," said Ruth. "April is nursing with us as well."

When she had attended to Angus, Ruth went over to find April and brought her to see her brother Will, who was also a little shocked to see his sister, but highly delighted. Once the wounds had been cleaned and dressed, they were feeling better; however, although the wounds were nasty, caused by gunshot, shrapnel and blade, they were not serious.

That evening, the friends, who were now resting, had a visit from April, Ruth and Paul. They talked about their reasons for being at the hospital and the disastrous charge. Further, they chatted about home. John said, "It will take us some time to recover, and quite honestly I think we have done our share of fighting."

April replied, "I believe you will soon be sent back to England to recuperate at home – we need room for more wounded men."

Will said, "I am sure the Light Brigade will not fight again in this war – the numbers left are so few."

"You are right," replied George, "and I for one don't see how with our wounds we will be able to stay in the Army."

Fred said, "I don't think any of us want to stay in the Army; we should carry on with our Engineering interests."

All agreed with these sentiments. Angus and Peter replied together, "Let's just get home and recover from this horror."

Ruth talked to her brother Angus. "I have fallen in love with Paul. I believe we will get married once the war is over."

"I am very glad for you. Bring him up home as soon as you can." The conversation ended when the order for lights out was shouted down the wards.

After a week in the hospital, all walking wounded were to be transported by ship back to Portsmouth. The Charge of the Light Brigade had caused two hundred and seventy-eight casualties and the Brigade would not see further action. The Earl of Cardigan, who had led the charge from the front, took part in the fight, then returned up the valley alone without bothering to rally or find out what had happened to the survivors. He left the field and boarded his yacht in Balaclava harbour, where he ate a champagne dinner.

On their return to their barracks, the troopers who had been wounded were given the option to stay in the army to recover, or to be retired and return home. The option was obvious for the friends: they had done their duty and served their Queen and country. They all agreed that war is a terrible thing and should be avoided, whenever possible; they had suffered themselves and seen the results of a horrific war.

The officer commanding the barracks, Major Newton, thanked them for their service in the officers' mess and wished them good luck. The next morning, after a hearty breakfast, the retired officers said a rather sad farewell to their comrades, then set off for their homes. The regiment said they could keep their uniforms in memory of their service. Further, the army provided carriages to transport them home, as their wounds did not permit them to ride. For Fred, Peter and John, it was less than a day's journey, Will had a full day of travel, whilst George and Angus had overnight stops at coaching inns.

The troopers of the 11th Hussars who remained in the barracks were soon sent to India to join the rest of the regiment already there. The regiment served with distinction in India for eleven years (1866-77), and later in the Gordon Relief Expedition with the Light Camel Regiment (1884). Subsequently, they fought in the First Boer War (1890) and in the First World War (1914-18), followed by the Second World War (1939-45).

The days of the cavalry regiments were soon to end, although they did take part in the First World War. Some regiments such as the Household Cavalry can still be seen on duty in London.

Chapter 7
1856

It was a joyous occasion: the war was over, and all over the country, in villages and towns, there were celebrations, particularly where the men had returned safely from the slaughter. Unfortunately, many men did not return, while others returned with severe injuries which caused hardship for them and their families. The war left fatherless children with mothers who were widows at an early age. Times were hard, widows had to find work and children started work very young. Fortunately, new companies were starting up, giving new opportunities to the general populace.

April had nursed a young officer from the Scots Greys who was also wounded at the Battle of Balaclava. A Scot from Edinburgh, he had been studying law at the university before joining the regiment, thinking, like many others, it would be a great adventure. Colin Stewart and April had become very close and fallen in love. They promised they would be together when the war ended. He had soon recovered from some nasty leg and arm cuts, partly due to the attention from April. On recovering, he was sent back to fight again in the Battle of Inkerman, where he was slightly wounded again. He was patched up and ended the war at the Siege of Sevastopol. Before the regiment returned to Scotland, Colin, now a Captain, went back to the hospital and met April. After an embrace and a long kiss, they went out for a meal together in Constantinople, where they agreed to meet up in Ironbridge as soon as possible on their return to Britain.

Ruth and Paul had decided to get engaged as soon as they returned to England. They had both promised Florence Nightingale they would help set up the first Training School for nurses at St Thomas's Hospital in London.

On arrival in England, Ruth and Paul made their way to London by coach, to spend a few days together before returning to their homes. Paul said, "I will buy you a ring in Garrards the Jewellers; after that, we will have to find some place to live, if possible near the hospital."

"Maybe we could have a meal out this evening and go to the theatre," replied Ruth."

"Good idea," said Paul.

The beautiful ring had a diamond centre with a ruby each side; it was to remind them that they had fallen in love amongst the carnage of war. They were very lucky in finding a spacious apartment not far from the hospital in a quiet area. It had just been vacated by an Army Major's family who were heading to India. Fully furnished and in good condition, it was ideal, so they placed a down payment so they could move in straight away. They retrieved their luggage from the hospital porter's lodge and left them at the apartment. Dinner was had at a local restaurant and then on to the Old Vic to see *Hamlet*. They returned to the apartment very tired but very happy. That night they expressed their love and enjoyed an intimate relationship.

Within a fortnight they had to report at the hospital, where Paul would work on the wards and Ruth would teach in the nurses' school. However, they decided they would travel to Kendal to meet Paul's family, then on to Ormiston to meet the McDonalds and get married.

After hiring a small coach and horse, they set off a day later in glorious weather, reaching Kendal late in the evening of the next day. Paul's family lived in a large house near the river in Kendal. His father was also a doctor. What a welcome they had after being away for nearly three years. They met Ruth, who showed them her engagement ring, and they all said they were happy for them and the life they had picked in London.

During dinner, Ruth said, "We are to get married in Ormiston before we return to London. Do you think you could get up for the wedding?"

"We will do our very best. Just let us know by telegram when it will be," replied Robert Ransome.

Paul's sister Mary and brother James had grown and were now sixteen and eighteen. He asked them if they knew what they were doing as careers. James said, "I love sailing and may go to Dartford College as a naval cadet."

"I love animals and would like to be a vet," was Mary's reply.

The next day they set off very early and travelled up to Ormiston in their carriage. It was late evening when they got to the hall, but they were just in time for dinner and another very happy meeting with the McDonalds. They were ushered in by Fergus to introduce Paul to the family. Ruth told them, "We have come home to be married. Just a simple ceremony, as we don't have much time."

"No such thing! That is wonderful – you will have a proper wedding, my dear," replied her mother Jean.

Paul was introduced to Ann and Hamish, who were now married and lived nearby; they had come over for dinner. Rose was also introduced. With her son Robert, who was now two, they had come over from Tranent to be there when Angus got home. Rose said, "I have received a telegram saying he will be home in the next few days, although he is still recovering from his wounds."

"You don't have to worry – he has a nurse and a doctor in the family now!" said Jean.

A good evening was had by all as they talked about the war and how Paul, Ruth and April had met the six friends in the hospital. Further, Jean was eager to start some plans for the wedding; however, it was late, so a decision was made to get the planning done in the morning – after all, Ruth was tired from the journey.

Angus arrived home the next day and was amazed to find a wedding was being planned. He was happy, however, for his sister and Paul, who had helped him in the hospital. His wounds were a lot better, so he agreed to be best man. How pleased he was to be home and to be greeted by the whole family. Rose said, "I am so happy to see you. I was so worried you might not return."

"Hello, Daddy," said little Robert.

"Well, hello to you. I am so glad to be back with you; maybe we should have a holiday together after the wedding, what do you think?"

"Yes," they both replied.

Within a week, the wedding had been arranged with the Church of Scotland in Ormiston; they knew the vicar well, and he had been most helpful. Telegrams had been sent to relatives and friends apologising for the short notice. The reception would be at the hall and a wedding dress had been bought in Edinburgh. Fred had arrived home and received a telegram; he was determined to go, and headed for Scotland. April, Colin and Will, likewise, would be at the wedding, and Paul's family were on their way. The other friends could not make it for they were still recovering.

The wedding went off well, with everyone having a good evening. Angus did his part as best man and was pleased to see his old friends and comrades, so a few drinks were dispensed with before the night was over. The next day, the young couple set off back to London as a married couple, to live in their apartment and work in the hospital. They would eventually have three children.

On her return to England, April soon made her way home to Ironbridge. Will had already arrived home and was recovering well from his wounds. The family were all delighted at their safe return. April explained how she had met and fallen in love with a young officer who had promised to come to Bridge Manor on his return.

Colin had returned to the Regimental Headquarters in Manchester with the troopers who had survived the war. He was asked to continue with the regiment, promoted to a Major and to return to the barracks in Edinburgh Castle. He thought hard about this: should he leave and continue his legal studies or make the Army his career. He decided he would be happy to return to his home city as second-in-command of the castle barracks.

Colin was given leave to return home before his new position commenced and would take time to travel to Ironbridge to see April. What a welcome he found as he was introduced to the Brown family. April told him about the wedding in Ormiston.

"I have been asked to take a post in Edinburgh Castle, so we could go up to Edinburgh and stay at Bruce House, my family home, as a base for the wedding."

"That would be marvellous," replied April. "Can Will come as well?"

"Of course, and we can spend some time together and meet my family."

April and Will had stayed at Colin's family home in Edinburgh for the wedding – Ormiston was only a short ride from Bruce House. They met the Stewart family. Colin's father, who had been a judge, had died the year before from a heart attack. His mother Mary and sister

Elisabeth, who was married to a Captain in the Gordon Highlanders called Walter McFarland, lived at the house. The house was a large five-bedroom on Royal Circus in Central Edinburgh, a stone's throw from the castle.

The day after the wedding, Colin proposed to April. "I love you very much; will you marry me and come to live with me in Edinburgh?"

"I thought you would never ask! Of course I will, my love." They embraced and kissed, then April said, "I would like to continue nursing."

"You could start a nursing school in the Edinburgh Hospital; they would no doubt welcome your help."

After a visit to Lennie, 46 Princess Street, which had just opened, April had been presented with a beautiful three-diamond cluster ring. The wedding would be arranged to take place in a month's time, and April would return home to Ironbridge to inform her parents and make preparations. Colin would report for duty and find a house for them in Edinburgh.

Back at Bridge House, her parents were overjoyed at the news. Samuel Brown, a Senior Staff Officer, was very pleased with his daughter's choice; he had heard of the bravery of the Scots Greys and admired Colin. Melissa Brown said, "At last, one of my girls is to be married. Come on, you three, we must make plans."

April and her sisters May and June were only too happy to help; the girls were excited as they discussed what they would wear as bride and bridesmaids.

The wedding took place on a lovely summer day in June; the ceremony was in the local parish church and the reception at the house and gardens. An invitation had been sent out to all the friends and family on both sides. This time, all the six friends were fit and well enough to attend. Colin was wearing his dress uniform, so the six friends wore their Hussar uniforms. Brigadier Brown led his daughter to the altar in his uniform. It was a resplendent affair with the colourful display of uniforms and beautiful dresses. What a night they had, the six comrades together again; they danced and drank their way into the early hours. During the evening, the friends had discussed what they would do in the future. Angus said, "I will look into improving the mining industry. What about you, Fred?"

"My ambition is to build steam ships and do away with sails."

"I want to study and build aircraft so we can fly to America," said Peter.

"That will never happen," replied George, "but the steam engines I design will improve our transport systems."

"I want to get involved with bridge building to enable your transport systems to exist," replied Will.

"Good for you!" John remarked. "I want to work on agricultural machines to aid the food industry and help save the workers from back-breaking labour."

"Well," finished Fred, "may I wish you all the best with your endeavours?" At that, they joined in the celebrations.

April and Colin headed for Oban for a brief honeymoon, returning to Edinburgh, where Colin had found a three-bedroom town house in a quiet area in Northumberland Street. They spent some time getting the house and furniture how they liked it, before they both had to return to work. Colin settled into his position at the castle and was pleased he could spend most of his evenings at home. April became well-known for her work at the Edinburgh Royal Infirmary setting up a new School of Nursing, which helped in establishing Edinburgh as a centre for good medical training. As time passed, they would have three children: two boys and a girl. They would always live in the city they loved, although they moved to a bigger house when the children were born.

Angus, who had fully recovered from his wounds, was almost back to full health, and would often visit the Stewart family with his wife Rose and little Robbie, as he was called. They became close friends.

Chapter 8
1858 – Angus

Angus and his family, Rose and Robbie, travelled to the popular seaside town of Scarborough for the holiday he had promised. They stayed at the Grand Hotel and had a restful time, which improved their relationship and helped Angus recover from the trauma of war. Robbie loved playing in the sand and going on the many rides; he particularly loved the swing boats and paddling in the sea.

Angus was now in charge of running the family coalmine and was conscious of improving the working conditions of the miners. He was determined to put his Engineering knowledge to work in the design and development of new, safer ways of mining.

The first coalmine was sunk in Scotland under the Firth of Forth in 1575. As the centuries continued, the population's dependence on coal increased and more mines were opened, but it was during the Industrial Revolution that coalmining burgeoned. Coal was used to power the massive steam engines as well as to create iron. It would take two tons of coal to make one ton of iron. Mining in Scotland was soon followed by mining villages opening in Lancashire, Yorkshire, South Wales, Northumberland and Durham. Whole populations of towns were dependent on employment from the mines.

The Mines and Collieries Bill was hastily passed by Parliament in 1842. The Act prohibited all underground work for women and girls and for boys under ten years. Further legislation in 1850 addressed the frequency of accidents in mines. The Coal Mines Inspection Act introduced the appointment of inspectors of coalmines, setting out their powers and duties, and placed them under the supervision of the Home Office.

There were two big engineering problems in mining coal underground: a system to drain water from the mine and a system to ventilate the mine and to provide fresh air to the miners. A special problem in coalmines was methane gas that sometimes accompanied coal, which could – and too often did – catch fire and explode. Protection for miners came with the invention of the Davy lamp and Geordie lamp, where any firedamp or methane burnt harmlessly within the lamp. It was achieved by preventing the combustion spreading from the light chamber to the outside air with either metal gauze or fine tubes. The illumination from such lamps was very poor.

Angus set about looking at these problems. Hand pumps were used to remove water, but this was hard work and often stopped the production of coal until most of the water was pumped away from the coal face. Early coalmines had a furnace at the bottom of a separate shaft.

The furnace created a draft and the draft ventilated the mine.

Angus had already designed a method of supporting the mine roof using steel instead of roofing timber, and was in the process of designing better methods of transporting the coal from the face. To improve the conditions and make his Ormiston mine more productive and at the same time improve the lot of miners throughout Britain, he needed an engineering manufacturing company. Steam, he decided, was the answer – he must design and build steam engine facilities that could pump out water and replace the furnaces with fans driven by steam engines. To do this, he would contact his friend George, who was already developing steam engines for the rail network. Further, he would look for capital to start his own engineering company to put his designs into practice. He approached his father, Fergus, who he persuaded to help him. Fergus kindly said, "I like the idea and I will approach other mine owners to be shareholders in the new company."

Angus got the capital he required, appointed an experienced miner from the mine as manager and set about recruiting men to work in the new company. They decided to call the company BMEC, short for British Mining Engineering Company. Angus managed to recruit some skilled men who had been working in Edinburgh, so they were happy to work nearer their homes. He took on some young lads to train; they would be taught by the older men. They started working on the new roof supports in a disused textile mill. The mill they bought was quickly turned into an Engineering workshop.

Angus contacted George to ask his advice on the design of steam engines for the mining industry. George was only too happy to help; his main interest now was building steam engines, and his expertise was second to none. His company had already produced many steam engines for different applications. The two friends soon had plans drawn up to apply steam engines to pump out water and run fans to create air currents and circulate air to ventilate a mine. Another application was the production of steam-driven conveyor systems to transport the coal quickly and safely. These applications, harnessing the power of steam, would increase the productivity of the mines and make them safer for the miners.

The new company went from strength to strength and was soon selling products at home and abroad. A purpose-built factory was constructed near the old one which required more staff, and many local people would gain a living from the new company.

During this time, Fergus McDonald had died, so the three family firms were now run by Angus, who saw that good managers were in place and the working men were fairly paid for their labours.

Angus was now head of the household at Ormiston Hall. Rose gave birth to three more children. A boy, Kenneth, was born in 1858, followed by a girl, Mary, in

1860, and their last child in 1861, another girl, Flora. Rose was advised by the doctor not to have any more children due to having high blood pressure.

Jean McDonald lived to see her last grandchild born to her son Angus and his wife Rose. The same year, while out riding, she was caught in a bad storm and was absolutely drenched. This led to a bad cold that turned into pneumonia and she unfortunately died. It was a sad time for all the family.

The textile company and mine company founded by Fergus prospered and did well with the introduction of new machines. The company founded by Angus, BMEC, was instrumental in helping the mine to greater profits. Other companies had sprung up manufacturing textile machinery, which helped to modernise the textile company and also make more profits. BMEC was a leader in its field, making a large income for Angus.

With the increase in income, the family were able to have holidays on the continent. They were able to purchase a holiday home near Nice on the French Riviera. The children loved their holidays, especially when they were at boarding school.

Angus became a well-known figure in Scotland, was respected by his employees and loved for his beneficent ways.

Chapter 9
1858 – George

George had returned to Belsay Hall in Northumberland, where his family were overjoyed at his safe arrival. His injuries from the war took some time to heal; the gash to his shoulder healed well, but the shot removed from his leg had damaged the muscle, so took longer to heal. He would always walk with a slight limp, although it was not long before he was riding again.

Caroline often came to see him as he recovered, which renewed their relationship: they were very much in love. George said, "I love you and want to marry you. Will you marry me?"

"Of course I will. I have been waiting for your return so I could hear those very words. You will have to ride into the village with me and ask my father, Dr Grant, for my hand in marriage."

Dr Grant was very happy to give George his approval to marry his daughter; he was the Armstrongs' family doctor and had seen George into the world. He knew his daughter would be well cared for and would be provided with all she needed.

George and Caroline had a trip down to Newcastle, where thy bought an engagement ring at Reid and Sons. It was a solitaire diamond set in gold. They celebrated with a nice meal in Fenwicks' restaurant and talked about the wedding and where they should live. "I think we should look for a house in Newcastle, where it would be easier for me to get to the company," George told Caroline.

"Yes, it would be nice to live in the city. I would love that."

The Grant family were all busy for the next couple of months preparing for the wedding. Caroline wanted to be married in the parish church where she had been christened. George said, "We should have the reception at Belsay Hall." So it was agreed they would make ready and send out invitations to all their friends and relatives.

George was now working for the family engineering company, getting more and more involved with his love of steam engines. The company had men who had worked for them since they were apprentices, so they had a skilled workforce developing new products. When George was approached by Angus, he was eager to help his friend and manufacture the steam engines he needed to develop the mining and textile industries. However, he was interested in the prospect of working on the steam locomotives, so applied to a local company, Robert Stephenson and Company.

Robert's father, George Stephenson, was born on 9th June 1781 in Wylam, Northumberland, which is nine miles from Newcastle-upon-Tyne. He was the second child of Robert and Mabel Stephenson, neither of whom could read or write. Robert was a fireman at Wylam Colliery, earning a very low wage, so there was no money for schooling. At seventeen, George became an engineman at Water Row Pit in Newburn nearby. He realised the value of education and paid to study at night school to learn reading, writing and arithmetic. He was illiterate until the age of eighteen years. Yet he became one of the great engineers of his era, a civil and mechanical engineer largely self-taught, a great example of diligent application and thirst for improvement. Renowned as the 'Father of the Railways', his chosen rail gauge – sometimes called the Stephenson Gauge – was the basis for the standard gauge used by most of the world's railways.

He pioneered rail transport, one of the most important technological inventions of the nineteenth century and a key component of the Industrial Revolution. Built by the Stephenson Company, the Locomotive No 1 was the first steam locomotive to carry passengers on a public line, the Stockton and Darlington Railway, in 1825. They also built the first public inter-city railway line in the world, the Liverpool and Manchester Railway, which opened in1830. From these early engineering achievements would grow the great British Railway network and the development of famous locomotives which would transform the lives of many people throughout the world.

Due to his experience and design knowledge, George was offered a senior position at the Stephenson Company. Henry Armstrong was not happy that his son was leaving their company; however, he knew his son was interested in locomotives, and George promised to return after a few years.

The wedding of George and Caroline took place as planned. For this wedding all the old friends were able to come up to Belsay Hall. It was a happy occasion. Will was the best man, and the bride looked lovely as she was given away by her father. At the hall, the reception want off without a hitch. The friends had a chance to discuss their recent activities and what they were planning to do in the future. Dancing and drinking continued into the early hours till most were ready to turn in, feeling rather tipsy. A number of friends stayed overnight at the hall; others had booked into the local hotel. George and Caroline went off early to head for their honeymoon in Italy: they had booked a holiday at the Grand Hotel on Lake Garda.

The couple found a suitable house in a nice area called Eldon Square in central Newcastle, not far from the company offices where George would work and within easy reach of schools and the main shopping area. They settled well into their new home and soon had a family of three children: two boys, Henry and George, and a girl, Ruth. They lived there for eight years until, unfortunately, Henry Armstrong died and George and his family moved into Belsay Hall so that George, the eldest son, could look after the estate and take over the running of the family company.

During the time George spent working with the Stephenson Company, he was instrumental in designing a number of new locomotives and seeing them through to production. Due to his work, the basic engineering principles that he established were later used to produce the great locomotives such as the Mallard and the Flying Scotsman. The rail network throughout the British mainland made passenger travel and the transportation of goods much easier. The technology soon spread throughout the Empire and the world, keeping many companies producing the rails and rolling stock in business and their workforce employed.

George took over the running of the family company with his brother Graham, who also had been to Cambridge and was now a qualified Engineer. They spent a number of years expanding the company and would welcome new ideas from their workforce. Many of their workforce had grown up with the company and would help to run the various departments. The Armstrong company would eventually be involved in making weapons and would become a well-known name in industry. They would form other companies such as the Armstrong Steel Company and Armstrong Steam Manufacturing Co. Ltd..

Chapter 10
1858 – Will

Will had recovered quickly from his battle wounds; the cut across his chest had only needed a few stitches and the shot in his thigh was not deeply embedded. He had returned home to work in the family foundries; however, his interest was in Bridge Building and other structures. In association with the railway industry, he set about designing bridges and railway station buildings from cast iron and later from steel.

Will was never that interested in girls, maybe because he had three sisters; he did, however, have other close relationships which were very good friends. He never married, but shared a house with a group of friends near Ironbridge. His sisters all married and had children who he adored, and they in turn loved Uncle Will, who would always bring them presents when he visited them. Grandfather Brown was now in poor health and had to retire from running the foundries. His son Samuel was a senior officer in the British Army, so the control of the company was Will's inheritance and was passed on to him with the understanding that some shares would be in the hands of other members of the family. The husband of his sister, Bill Cooper, was a manager at the factory in Wellington, later to become Telford, where the company had built a new factory when demands for their products increased. As Will was spending a lot of time in bridge design and was gaining an interest in bridge building, he decided to appoint managers in the companies at Ironbridge and Wellington, reporting to a newly formed board of directors which included his father, grandfather, Bill and other shareholders. Will would, of course, keep an eye on the progression of the company, which had expanded and was doing good business.

Will, who was now well-known in the engineering industry for his knowledge of materials, was immediately employed by one of Thomas Telford's companies. He had studied applied mechanics in relation to structures and his structural knowledge of shear forces, bending moments and beam calculations was advanced.

Thomas Telford was born at Glendinning, a hill farm three miles east of Eskdalemuir in the rural parish of Westerkirk in Eskdale, Dumfriesshire. His father, a shepherd, died soon after his birth, and his mother raised him in poverty. At the age of fourteen, he was apprenticed to a stonemason and studied architecture in his spare time. After a time working in Edinburgh, he moved to London, where he met and was influenced by Robert Adam and Sir William Chambers. There he was involved in building additions to Somerset House. Later, he found work at Portsmouth dockyard and although largely self-taught, was extending his talents to the

117

specification, design and management of building projects. Through his wealthy patron, William Pulteney, he became Surveyor of Public Works in Shropshire. He built many highways and bridges – forty in Shropshire, such as the bridge carrying the London to Holyhead road over the River Severn at Montford. Other notable bridges were the Conwy and Menai suspension bridges.

Thomas Telford, FRS, FRSE, after establishing himself as an engineer of road and canal projects in Shropshire, designed numerous projects in his native Scotland, as well as harbours and tunnels. Such was his reputation as a prolific designer of highways and related bridges, he was dubbed the 'Colossus of Roads'. Reflecting his command of all types of civil engineering, he was elected the first President of the Institution of Civil Engineers, a post he held for fourteen years until his death. The town of Telford in Shropshire was named after him – a truly remarkable man.

When Will joined the Thomas Construction Group, his main aim was to establish himself as a structural steel bridge builder and to gain knowledge of all aspects of manufacture and construction techniques. Will worked for the company for a number of years, gaining an insight into current practices and then forming new ideas in bridge building as steel structural sections became available. He was responsible for designing, manufacturing and constructing bridges throughout the country for both road and rail. This was an era when men of vision paved the way in establishing new ideas that led to the formation of the engineering institutions. Will and his colleagues at the company formed groups of engineers with similar interests to meet up and discuss their problems and successes. This would be happening in other parts of the country and would eventually lead in later years to the formation of the Institution of Structural Engineers.

Will left the Thomas Construction Group to return to his own companies; this was after the company offered him a promotion to the board so that he would stay, as they valued his hard work. On his return, he was then in a position both technologically and financially to build another factory with state-of-the-art machines and equipment to manufacture steel structures and bridges. The William Brown Structural Group would become known throughout the Empire for manufacturing and supplying bridges and relevant structures to both rail and road-building industries.

One notable bridge was the Clifton Suspension Bridge spanning the Avon Gorge. It links Clifton in Bristol to Leigh Woods in North Somerset and is one of the first of its kind ever built. The bridge is built to a design by William Henry Barlow and John Hawkshaw, although it was based on an earlier design by Isambard Kingdom Brunel. The steelwork was manufactured by the William Brown Structural Group and other companies, the construction was completed in 1864 and became a distinctive landmark, a great achievement in its day.

Will never had a family of his own; however, his three sisters had children who would inherit his companies and his fortune, which was built up due to his hard work and engineering ability. Will, like his other friends, would keep in touch and on occasion meet up at social and regimental events. After the sad death of his father, Will took over the running of Bridge Manor, although for a number of years while he was away working on different projects the estate was run by a manager. The manager had worked for his father, who was often away on military business, and the house was left in control of his mother, who had loyal servants to help her.

Will had understood that for his staff and workforce in his companies to work hard and to be loyal he had to see they had fair salaries and wages. This philosophy would exist throughout his three works, and he made sure his managers were aware of this, making people keen to work for him. He would make a point of visiting the works to meet his men and women and was a stern but fair owner. He played golf and was very interested in nature; he gave of his wealth to good causes helping the sick and poor.

Chapter 11
1858 – Fred

On his return to Chard House, Fred had a hero's welcome from the family and in particular a loving greeting from his wife June. "How happy I am to see you back safe and sound."

"Not quite sound yet," replied Fred. "This leg of mine is still not right."

"Well," said June, "meet your daughter Victoria, who is nearly four."

Little Vicky, as she became known, was rather shy at first. "My, you are a surprise and a big girl already. Come and tell me what you like doing."

Soon, Vicky became very close to her father and he loved her very much. Fred and June would go on to have another girl, Rebecca, and twin sons Simon and Paul.

Fred's leg wound took some time to heal, so he had time to enjoy family life for a short while. He soon, however, got thinking about his future activities and his ambition to build steam ships. He drew up plans at first for a small steamer to be used on rivers and lakes. The family shipbuilding company was a little against steel ships, so they required Fred to find out more about the construction techniques for building steam-powered, iron-hulled ships before they could invest in a new project. Fred found out that a company called John Scott Russell & Co were building an iron steamship called the SS *Great Eastern* at their yard on the River Thames. The ship was designed by Isambard Kingdom Brunel, which at that time was the largest ship ever built, with the capacity to carry four thousand passengers from England to Australia without refuelling. Fred was given the opportunity to work for the company and observe the building and outfitting skills needed to construct such a vessel. With his knowledge of shipbuilding from working with his family company, he was soon doing valuable work designing some of the many components required when building this great ship. His contribution to overseeing the installation of the steam engines, paddle wheels and screw propellers was noted by his superiors and he would be rewarded for his hard work.

Isambard Kingdom Brunel was born on 6th April 1806 in Britain Street, Portsea, Portsmouth, Hampshire, where his father was working. He was named Isambard after his father, French civil engineer Sir Marc Isambard Brunel, and Kingdom after his English mother, Sophia Kingdom. The family moved to London in 1808 for his father's work. Brunel had a happy childhood, despite the family's constant money worries. His father taught him drawing and observational techniques from the age of four, and by the age of eight he had learned Euclidean geometry; he also learned fluent French and the basic principles of engineering. He was encouraged to draw interesting buildings and identify any faults in their structure. He was sent to Dr Morrell's boarding school in Hove, where he learned classics. His father, a Frenchman by birth, sent Isambard at the age of fourteen first to the University of Cean, then to the Lycée Henri-IV in Paris.

When Brunel was fifteen, his father, who had accumulated debts of over £5000, was sent to a debtors' prison. After three months went by with no prospect of release, Marc Brunel let it be known he was considering an offer from the Tsar of Russia. In August 1821, facing the prospect of losing a prominent engineer, the government relented and issued Marc £5000 to clear his debts in exchange for his promise to stay in Britain. This turned out well, for it was Marc Brunel who was instrumental in the design and construction of the first tunnel under the River Thames, linking both sides by rail. The young Isambard worked for his father building the tunnel, which was dangerous work at the time. Many accidents occurred in the early days, until tunnelling techniques were improved. Unfortunately, Isambard was quite badly injured in a roof collapse and spent several months recovering, while some of his workmates lost their lives. He went on to become one of the most ingenious and prolific figures in civil engineering history, one of the nineteenth century's engineering giants. His work changed the face of the English landscape with his ground-breaking designs and ingenious constructions. Isambard built dockyards, the Great Western Railway, a series of steamships, including the first propeller-driven transatlantic steamship, and numerous important bridges and tunnels. His designs revolutionised public transport and modern engineering. He designed and built three ships that revolutionised naval engineering: the SS *Great Western* (1838), the SS *Great Britain* (1843) and the SS *Great Eastern* (1859). In 2002, Brunel was placed second in a BBC public poll to determine the '100 Greatest Britons'. He is remembered as one of the greatest engineers ever.

Fred met Isambard when he visited the shipyard during the building of the SS *Great Eastern*. Brunel knew the ship affectionately as the 'Great Babe'. He was at the launch, but died in 1859, shortly after her maiden voyage.

After some delays, the *Great Eastern* began her maiden voyage to North America on 17th June 1860. There were thirty-five paying passengers and eight company passengers, one of whom was Fred, who was rewarded for his work helping to build the ship. The ship's first transatlantic crossing went without incident, and she easily survived a small gale and arrived in New York on 28th June. Many vessels and tens of thousands of people flocked to see her arrive. Fred really enjoyed the relaxing journey and his first visit to the USA. After meeting many Americans, who showed great interest in the ship, one very rich shipbuilder tried to persuade Fred and some of his colleagues to start up a steel shipbuilding yard in the States. This for Fred was out of the question: he had plans of his own at home and a loving family waiting for his return. He decided to return to the UK by fast clipper, which was a dual passenger and goods vessel returning to its home port of Liverpool.

The SS *Great Eastern* left New York in late July, taking several hundred passengers on an excursion to Cape May and then to Old Point, Virginia. She would eventually ply the route between North America and Britain as a passenger liner for several years before being converted to a cable-laying ship. She laid the first lasting transatlantic telegraph cable in 1866, finishing her life as a floating music hall and advertising hoarding in Liverpool.

On his arrival back in Britain, Fred was greeted back with the knowledge of the birth of his second daughter and spent some time resting, before facing his family shipbuilding board. At the first board meeting after his return to the company, the members asked Fred if he would now take over control of the company from his father. Edward was now in poor health and would gradually retire as Fred took over the reins. Fred was willing to do this provided they agreed with his future plans to modernise the yard and build steel steamships. The members were pleased with Fred's report and were fully aware of his experiences, so agreed to give him the finances necessary to build a new generation of ships from a converted yard.

Fred was quick to learn of the need for new battleships for the Royal Navy, so he set about designing a steam-powered armoured frigate. Other countries were considering building steel warships, so when the Admiralty was approached with plans for a new frigate and a modern yard to build them, they were eager to seriously consider approval of a contract.

HMS *Warrior* is a forty-gun steam-powered armoured frigate built for the Royal Navy between 1859 and 1861. She was the name ship of the Warrior-class ironclads. *Warrior* and her sister ship HMS *Black Prince* were the first armour-plated, iron-hulled warships. After spending her active career with the Channel Squadron, she became obsolescent following the 1873 commissioning of the mastless and more capable HMS *Devastation*. She was placed in reserve and then decommissioned in 1883, when she served as a store ship and then was converted into an oil jetty in 1927. In 1979, she was donated to the Maritime Trust, where she was fully restored and returned to Portsmouth as a museum ship, listed as part of the National Historic Fleet.

With the contract from the Royal Navy, Fred's company prospered designing and building the new generation of warships. His fellow board members and shareholders were delighted with the new venture. The company went on to build not only warships but other ships for the merchant navy, including troop carriers.

Fred became the head of the family after the sudden death of his father. He managed the estate and the company until his retirement. His twin sons took over the running of the company; both had grown up with an interest in shipbuilding: Simon studied Naval Architecture and Paul Mechanical Engineering.

Chapter 12
1858 – Peter

Peter had a similar welcome to Fred on his return to Chard. They had grown up together and had become like brothers. His family lived in a cottage near the stables where his father was the manager; there he was welcomed with some relief by his parents and his sister Ellie. At the big house they met for a special meal to celebrate the safe return of their sons.

During the charge, Peter had been shot in the arm and leg, and a piece of shot had gone straight through his arm without much damage. His leg had a piece of shrapnel lodged in it which had to be removed by the army surgeon, which meant it was some time before he was fully fit. During this time, Jane Moore the baker's daughter renewed her acquaintance with Peter and spent many hours with him during his recovery. Once he recovered enough to be able to ride, they were often seen riding together on the estate and in the surrounding area. They became lovers as their attraction to each other had been reignited, and Jane said, "I fell in love with you the first time we met and therefore I was happy to wait for your return."

Peter replied, "I was in love with you; however, I did not want to get too involved at the time. If you will marry me, I will ask your father for your hand."

"Of course I will marry you, my darling; no one will stop me," Jane shouted with joy.

Mr Moore was very pleased with his daughter's choice and had wondered when Peter would propose. They went into London to Garrards the Jewellers, where Jane chose a beautiful sapphire and diamond ring for their engagement. The Shawcrofts said they could hold the reception for the wedding at Chard House, and they would be married by Father Doyle in the local Catholic church.

Invitations were sent out to all their friends and relations; all of Peter's comrades from university and the army replied to say they would be there to meet up and wish him well.

During his time of recuperation, one of Peter's visitors was John Stringfellow, who had allowed him to work in his aircraft building workshop. John knew of his interest in Aeronautic design and research, and therefore was eager to offer Peter a job as designer with the task of gathering all the knowledge he could from around the world. This would help the company to build the next generation of airplanes and keep ahead in the race to fly. Peter accepted his offer and agreed to start as soon as he was able and said in the meantime he would continue with his own ideas for manned flight.

The old friends all arrived to stay overnight before the wedding; those from the North, who had further to travel, would also stay after the wedding reception. Angus and George were invited to stay in Chard House; the others were put up in the Phoenix Hotel in Chard, where Peter had arranged a stag party for his friends. What a night they had. A special room was booked for their party, they had a good evening meal with plenty of local beer, and caught up on all their different ventures.

The wedding was a wonderful affair, with Fred acting as best man and Peter's sister Ellie and Fred's wife June and daughter little Victoria being among the bridesmaids. The reception had been arranged with great care at Chard House, with a delicious meal followed by the usual speeches and much jovial banter, ending with a dance and drinking to the small hours. The married couple went off early to get down to their honeymoon hotel in Brighton, where they would holiday for the next fortnight.

On their return, the couple moved into a farm cottage on the estate, vacated by a tenant farmer who had retired and moved to live with his daughter in Chard. Within a short time they had a new arrival who was named baby Jack, and a year later a baby girl named Rosemary. In time, they had six children – two boys and four girls – and they all did well, living happily in their cottage. Although Peter did earn a comfortable salary, he never wanted to move to a bigger house. He and his family loved living near the big house and the stables. Uncle

Fred and his family became very close as the years passed. The cottage was extended with more bedrooms and a bigger kitchen to accommodate the growing family.

John Stringfellow was an early British aeronautical inventor known for his work on the Aerial Steam Carriage with his partner William Samuel Henson. Born in Attercliffe, Sheffield, he moved to Chard in 1820 to work as a maker of bobbins and carriages for the lace industry. In 1827, he married Hannah Keetch and together they had ten children. With William Henson they started work in an old lace factory experimenting with model aircraft. They had ambitions of creating an international company, the Aerial Transit Company. After many experiments with Stringfellow's ideas centred on monoplane and triplane models and Henson's ideas on using steam power, in 1848 Stringfellow achieved the first powered flight using an unmanned ten-foot wingspan steam-powered monoplane named 'Ariel'.

In the light of recent research and developments, a number of history textbooks that present the view that the Wright Brothers invented powered flight are having to be changed and replaced with the true inventor, John Stringfellow of Chard. He should get the recognition he deserves for his achievement and the birthplace of the aviation industry we have today. In addition, the first flight of his vehicle 'Bat' in 1849 created the world's first Unmanned Air Vehicle (UAV). A bronze model of that first primitive aircraft stands in Fore Street in Chard. The town's museum has a unique exhibition of flight before the advent of the internal combustion engine and before the manned, powered flight made famous by the Wright Brothers.

Peter started working full-time for John Stringfellow and his company. He was happy for him to make models of the designs he had already drawn down. Many test flights were made, with some good results and many failures. Most of the developing countries were striving to be the first to achieve manned flight, so Peter was able to gather much information and knowledge which was put to use in further experiments. After much hard work and countless trials, a new company, Armstrong Design and Build Ltd (ADB), was founded with Peter as the managing director. Their developments in airframe design and aircraft flight control systems would enable them to undertake a manned flight. Although from early times man had experimented with flight and had been successful with lighter-than-air vehicles such as balloons, it was not until this era that man had had any success with heavier-than-air vehicles.

Using a steam-powered monoplane, ADB made one of the first manned flights. The company prospered building gliders and was one of the first companies to use the internal combustion engine to turn a propeller. Peter lived to see this, but by then his sons were running the company which he had founded and would eventually build aircraft for the Royal Flying Corps in the First World War.

Chapter 13
John – 1858

On his return to Longmeadows from the hell of the Crimean War, John had a hero's welcome from his family and the opportunity to recover from his wounds. He had received severe cuts to his arm and leg, so the prospect of a comfortable bed and clean dressings was indeed most welcome. However, a shock awaited him. When he asked one of the servants called Bill to run over to ask Grace to visit him, he knew there was something wrong by the expression on his face. "What is the matter, Bill? Please tell me."

"I am afraid Grace had a fatal accident. I am so sorry, sir, but she died and was buried a few months ago."

John was shattered by the news. Grace had been working in the hayloft on the farm when she had slipped and fell onto an old plough that had been left below, receiving injuries from which she died instantly.

It took some time for John to recover from his heartbreak at losing Grace and for his wounds to heal. His sister June would visit and the family did their best to help him. John said he would tour the farms on their land and do his best to improve the working conditions and safe working. His interest in farming machinery was renewed as he recovered, and he designed machines that could save time and hence money. He decided he would start his own company when he could, but at first he would apply to work for one of the emerging agricultural engineers. During this time of recovery, his sister would visit him and bring along Peter's sister Ellie, who had grown into a beautiful young lady. John soon became very fond of Ellie and she of him. It was clear that this mutual alliance was helping John to become his old self again, to the relief of his family.

Once John was fit to ride, he did tour the farms and required the farmers to make improvements that made working conditions safer. He became a regular visitor at Chard House, where Ellie had become part of the family. The two families at Chard were very much like one family: they had dinner together at least once a week and Ellie was like a daughter to Melissa Shawcroft. The relationship between John and Ellie grew until they found they were in love. They had been out riding one Sunday after Mass – John would often make an effort to visit Ellie on a weekend. After riding for some time, they came to the River Yarty and dismounted at a very quiet spot where it was deep enough to swim. It was a warm summer's day. "Can you swim?" asked John.

"I love swimming; we learned to swim in the lake on the estate," said Ellie. "What about you?"

"I learned to swim in our lake and in the River Rother which led into it."

"Come on then, let's go for a swim."

So, in wild abandon they undressed with some modesty and splashed into the river. After some swimming and a little horseplay, they embraced in the water, which led to intimate lovemaking. "I love you, Ellie; will you become my wife?" asked John.

"I have liked you since we first met when you were a Cavalry Officer; however, I was very young then and you went off to war. Now, darling, I love you with all my heart, and the answer is yes. Kiss me!"

On their return to the Chard Estate, John went to see Jack Archer in the stable yard and asked for Ellie's hand in marriage. Jack and the family were all delighted with their daughter's choice.

The next day they went into Chard and bought a beautiful solitaire diamond ring for their engagement, and, after a light lunch back at Chard House, they made their way to Longmeadows to announce their engagement to the Cromwell family, who were equally pleased. The wedding was arranged for mid-summer's day. The Shawcrofts were happy for them to have the reception at Chard House. The wedding ceremony would take place in the family Catholic church; although John had been brought up as a Protestant, he was very happy with the arrangements. He said, "Being a Christian is what is important, not which building you worship in."

Ransomes, Sims and Jefferies Limited had been founded as an agricultural machinery maker. Their base was set up in 1845 in Ipswich and was named Orwell

Works. John had approached them with his new ideas; they had been delighted with his designs and he was asked to join the company immediately. The common tools of farming were the plough and the sickle, which were often made by the local blacksmith. With the aid of John's designs, the company were able to produce horse-drawn reapers and ploughs. Later, they would manufacture tilling equipment and an early combine harvester. John worked for the company for three years, becoming the Production Manager with a good salary, and this gave him the experience he needed to set up his own company close to his home near Midhurst. Although Ransomes did not like the idea of John leaving them, they came to an agreement that if John would act as their Agent in the south, they would help to fund the start-up of his company.

John managed to find some old blacksmith's building, a mile from his home at Longmeadows, which came with five acres of land. A gradual building programme commenced which would provide the workshops for the new agricultural engineering company. John employed men from the local area; some had been blacksmiths or farm labourers, and a few skilled men moved down with him from Ipswich. The company was simply called AEC Ltd.

It was a few days before the wedding of John and Ellie; invitations had been sent out and friends and relatives had started arriving from different parts of the UK. The age of steam had arrived, which meant travelling long distances was much easier. However, arrangements had to be made to collect people from the stations; therefore the horses and coaches were in great demand. John had asked Fred, his brother-in-law, to be his best man, while the girls in the family of Peter and Fred would be bridesmaids. Fred, however, was on his way back from the USA, hoping to arrive back in time.

The other friends had arrived safely and had gathered together with some male relatives for a stag night at the local hotel. A good meal had been consumed and the drinks were flowing when the door to their room burst open and in walked Fred, to the relief of John. Fred was a little weary due to his ride from Liverpool, but nevertheless he joined in, describing his adventures on the new steamship. They all had news to tell about their work, which led to the main topic of conversation being the use of steam engines. The night out ended when they decided John had had enough and managed to carry him to the coach to get him home.

The following morning turned out to be a warm summer's day, after a terrible night of thunder and lightning. The church service passed without incident, with the reception being a very happy occasion. The only problem during the evening was when a cousin of Ellie's and Angus got into a rather heated debate about religion; however, Fred was at hand and persuaded them to agree to differ. He told them, "This is not the time or the place to fall out over doctrine; every man is entitled to his opinion, and is it that important anyway?"

The dancing and drinking went on till late, but by then the new married couple had gone off on their honeymoon to Paris.

On their return from Paris, after a wonderful time, they would live at Longmeadows. Robert Cromwell was not very well, which meant John had to take on more responsibility for the estate. However, his business was taking up a lot of his time, so he appointed a manager. The man was a farmer's son known to the family who had done well at agricultural college and was ideal for the job. Later that same year, a son, Andrew, was born to the couple, and this was followed as the years passed with three daughters and another son. Andrew would take over running the estate as John got older. Andrew was more interested in farming rather than engineering; on the other hand, the youngest son, Richard, loved working at the engineering company and grew up to become the Managing Director when his father retired.

The company AEC Ltd prospered as new machines were designed, manufactured and sold, first in the south of England, then throughout the UK and eventually worldwide. John used his designs to incorporate steam engines, manufacturing from his foundry and workshops a new range of portable steam-powered ploughing and threshing machines. The early ploughing machines were used in pairs, placed on either side of a field to haul a plough back and forth between them using a wire cable. This early work led to the company making one of the first farm tractors and even tanks in the First World War.

All this would lead to the sophisticated agricultural machinery produced in later years.

Chapter 14
1900

A final meeting of the friends took place at a reunion of survivors of the now historical 'Charge of the Light Brigade'. Those present were old men, mostly retired or at the end of their active lives. Only four of the friends were to meet, as both Angus and Will had died. Angus, at the age of sixty-eight and not in the best of health, had gone for a hike in Glencoe. The weather had been perfect as he ventured out with his now-adult children; however, as is often the case in the mountains, the weather turned and they were absolutely soaked to the skin. On their return home to Ormiston, Angus came down with a cold that turned to pneumonia, which led to his death.

Will had retired at sixty-seven. After running a very successful business, he had retired to his home in Ironbridge to look after his partner, who had become ill with consumption (TB). This led to Will contracting the disease and within two years both had died.

The friends had great success in their lives due to study and hard work, and all had contributed to the future technological age, passing on their knowledge to the generations to follow.

As they remembered their old friends, Fred proposed a toast. "To our old friends and comrades, may they never be forgotten."

George replied, "To us all, and God bless the Queen," to which they all replied:

"God bless the Queen."